Winning Her Love

Rocky Mountain Christmas Train
Book One

Katie O'Connor

Snarky Heart Press

Winning Her Love

Katie O'Connor

—Winning Her Love—

—Rocky Mountain Christmas Train, Book One—

Published November 2024 by Snarky Heart Press and Katie O'Connor

(katieohwrites.com)

ISBN: 978-1-989816-89-9 Digital Edition 1

ISBN: 978-1-989816-87-5 Digital Edition 2

ISBN: 978-1-989816-91-2 (Print Edition)

Cover art by Kelly Moran

Copyediting by Terri St. Clair

Dedication

This one is for my train pals. Roxy, Shawna, Raine, and Ellen.
Ladies it's been a fun ride.
This story is for my three biggest fans,
my mother, Irene, my sister, Jean,
and my unofficially adopted sister
and number one fan, Suzette.
Love you all muchly.

Winning Her Love

Joy Spencer is an overprotective mother to seven-year-old Chantal, who lives with cerebral palsy. They're on the Christmas train to raise money for the Cerebral Palsy Association. She's prepared to do anything to win, except put her daughter in danger.

Seth Mathison is a firefighter on a mission to earn money for the Alberta Children's Hospital Burn Unit. Since his niece's death, he's separated himself from family and friends and isn't great with children. When young Chantal Spencer starts following him around on the train, he doesn't know how to get rid of her. She makes him nervous. He's certain she'll get hurt the way she's lurching around on the moving train. He doesn't need that on his conscience.

When Seth and Joy are thrust together to serve as supervisor and emcee of a local choir's Christmas pageant, Seth suggests that Chantal substitute for a sick cast member. Joy is irate. There's no way on this earth that she'll subject her daughter to possible failure and humiliation.

Will their anxieties ruin everything, or will the miracle of Christmas help them get beyond their biases and fears and find true love?

The News Post

Charity Train Rolls This December.

Win the trip of a lifetime this December on the maiden voyage of the luxurious Rocky Mountain Christmas Train. With a chance to win a $25,000 cash prize for the charity of your choice. To enter, send your name, address, and a bio, along with the name of your charity and why you chose it to 3566 Maple Lane, Delta, Alabama, 36258.

Chapter One

Relief fluttered through his stomach as Seth Mathison eased through the crowded terminal and onto his designated platform. Thank heaven he hadn't missed the train. A snowstorm had delayed his flight from Calgary. Then they'd circled the Denver airport seven times before getting the clearance to land. He'd be beyond annoyed and sorely disappointed if he missed this chance.

He struggled to be patient in the motionless crowd. What in the world was the holdup?

His heart jumped, and he sighed with relief when he spotted the gaily lit train over the heads of the crowd. Bright holiday lights were strung along the length of each car of the long train. He'd done his research. The train had fifty cars, some were new and some were refurbished. These included luxurious sleeper cars, three different dining cars, three parlor cars, a library, two kitchens, three observation cars including one double-decker, a lounge car, and staff accommodations.

He fingered his tweed overcoat's pocket to ensure his pre-paid ticket was still there. He'd lucked out when his entry was chosen. What a great opportunity to let the world know about the dangers of home fires. If, no, when he won, he'd donate the twenty-five-thousand-dollar prize to the burn unit at The Alberta Children's Hospital. Presenting that much money would give him media attention too, and that would help inform people of the danger of home fires. This was about saving lives.

Being away from work for a full month didn't bother him. His deputy chief was more than capable of handling the station in his absence. Learning that his travel expenses were covered by the contest was a bonus, though he'd have come anyway, just for the publicity. This was an opportunity too big to pass up. Nothing mattered more than fire safety.

As *We Wish You a Merry Christmas* played over the train depot's speakers, the crowd sang along. How many of these people were going on the train? Surely not all of them. There had to be five hundred people here jostling each other about. They certainly weren't fitting that many people on this train. Of course, Denver was a major stopping point.

How many other trains use this depot? Were most of these people saying goodbye to loved ones? Waiting for another train? He glanced at his watch again. It was just after eight a.m. and departure time was listed as eight-fifteen. What were they waiting for? Shouldn't they be boarding by now? He searched the crowd for someone, anyone, who looked like they might be in charge.

The speaker crackled, and the music ended with a screech that impaled his eardrums. Too many decibels for safety. He shook his head to clear the ringing in his ears.

"Ladies and gentlemen, welcome to The Rocky Mountain Christmas Train's first annual Christmas Charity Dream Trip. Are you ready to board?"

The crowd's roar was deafening. He should have worn earplugs. Find the positive, he reminded himself. His niece, Gwyn, would have told him to look for the bright spot. Since she wasn't here, he tried to adopt her positive mindset despite his exhaustion.

The positive here was that he'd won the opportunity to be on the train and compete for the grand prize. All prizes were awarded to a pre-approved charity. He'd labored for hours over his entry form. Now, here he was, boarding the train and ready to compete. Luck had definitely been in his favor, as rumor had it that tens of thousands of people had entered the Canada-U.S. wide contest.

"If you flip to the second page of your ticket package," a female voice announced, "you'll find your car and room numbers. Please make your way to your car and board in an orderly fashion after placing your baggage on the carts provided. Our staff is happy to load your baggage for you."

He looked at his snowy white ticket's bright red and green print. No doubt custom-designed for the inaugural journey. A souvenir for sure. He was in car number eighteen. Assuming they were in numerical order, and why wouldn't they be, he headed left, toward the front of the train.

In keeping with the season, the crowd moved gently. There was almost no pushing and shoving. Everyone was cheerful and polite. Until he reached car nineteen when someone shouted, "Get out of my way. Can't you move any faster than that?"

A woman's high-pitched voice shouted back. "Just be patient. She's going as fast as she can. What kind of grinch are you that you can't give a physically disabled child thirty seconds to board a holiday train? You should be ashamed of yourself."

He could almost see her shaking her finger in the man's face. Good for her. Children were precious and needed protection from the ugly realities of life. The crowd parted, and he had a clear view of the altercation.

A burly man in his mid-forties glared down at a petite woman and her child. The blonde had her arm wrapped protectively around the shoulders of a girl with arm crutches. "Look, lady," the man snapped. "I paid big money to ride this train and no little snip of a woman, and her damaged goods child are going to keep me from my berth."

Seth hadn't realized that the train would have paying customers as well as contestants. That was neither here nor there. The man should be more patient.

"She is not damaged goods," the woman declared. "She has cerebral palsy. The only person who is damaged here is you, you deranged galloot."

"Lady, you're testing my patience."

What kind of man acted like that? He was a big bully. Seth stepped forward to stand up for the woman, though he admired her spunk.

"Sir, if it wasn't Christmas, I'd tell you exactly what I think of you," the woman proclaimed. "But Christmas is the time of love and caring, I'll just ask you to step aside so we can board. We *were* here before you."

The man's face turned florid. Seth stepped between the combatants. "Stand down, sir. Give the family a moment to board." The man was tall but not as tall as Seth. He blustered a bit and stepped back with a sarcastic bow. Seth said, "We appreciate your patience. Go ahead, Ma'am. Take your time."

"Thanks," she said. "We appreciate you stepping in, but I had it handled. I might be a single mother, but I am capable of taking care of my child." She smiled, spun round, and taking her daughter by the arm, assisted her up the tall steps onto the train. The young girl flashed Seth a smile.

Rocky Mountain Christmas Train

Chapter Two

"Take your time, Chantal," Joy Spencer told her daughter as they made their way toward their sleeping quarters.

"Mama, I could have waited to get on the train," Chantal said over her shoulder. Her waist-length blonde hair swung across the back of her bulky down jacket. California was a long way from Denver, and they'd had to buy special winter clothing for this trip of a lifetime. Thank heaven for secondhand stores.

"You shouldn't have to wait," Joy grumbled. "People need to be more patient."

Chantal laughed. "Mama, you are being very impatient right now. Everyone is just excited. If I could run down the aisle, I would, I'm so happy." She giggled.

"You're too kind to people who should be more tolerant." Joy sighed. Chantal was fragile. She'd been diagnosed with spastic cerebral palsy just after her third birthday. The diagnosis had broken Joy's heart, but Chantal had taken it in stride, so to speak. She was a veritable Pollyanna and not nearly cautious enough to suit Joy, who worried every moment her daughter was out of her sight. "And that man didn't need to butt in."

"Mama, he was being kind. He was handsome too, wasn't he?" At seven, Chantal had decided she needed a new father since hers had abandoned them, and the ever-growing mountain of medical bills when Chantal was diagnosed.

"I suppose so, but I've told you, more than once, I don't have time for men." He had been handsome. Tall, probably over six feet, with dark hair and eyes. His jacket looked expensive. He was probably one of the tourists on the train rather than a contestant. She pushed his image out of her head. She was here to win the prize, not get caught up in a man, no matter how handsome.

Gosh, she felt like a Grinch today. She needed to lighten up. This trip was dual purpose. A free vacation and a chance to win enough money to pay off Chantal's medical bills. As a receptionist at a veterinary clinic, she didn't make nearly enough to live on and pay down their massive debts. If they won, they'd pay off their debts and donate any leftovers to the Cerebral Palsy Association. She'd have been lost without their guidance and support.

"Here it is!" Chantal almost wobbled over in her excitement when her crutches tangled together.

Joy forced a smile. "Careful there." She barely resisted the urge to steady her daughter. Instead, she handed over the digital key to their accommodations so Chantal could unlock the door. She held her breath as Chantal slid her arm out of the crutch's cuff, rested the crutch against the wall, and stuck the key in the slot. Joy clenched her fists to keep them still. She'd never get used to Chantal taking even the smallest risk.

Chantal pushed open the door and gasped. "Mama, it's beautiful." She grabbed her crutch and stumbled inside, oohing and aahing as she went.

Joy followed and eased the door shut behind them. She gasped in delight equal to her daughter's. She'd been expecting a utilitarian room with nothing more than bunk beds. This was the height of luxury. Decorated in cream and navy, it was practically a suite. Over in the corner, there was a table with two chairs. There was a bar fridge, and a pair of plush twin beds piled high with pillows. There was even a tiny bathroom with a shower. "Wow. This is amazing."

There was a tall thin tree lit with blazing multi-color lights in one corner. A garland of silver stars hung over the window. Outside, snow drifted down on the busy platform. It was a holiday dream.

Now, if only her dreams of winning this contest would come true. They could be free and clear...at least until the next disaster.

The bags they had sent ahead were set under the tree like presents. There was a cream-colored envelope with gold script on one of the beds. Joy picked it up and ran her fingernail under the seal.

Dear Joy and Chantal:

Please join us in the forward observation car at 9:15 a.m. for an introduction to your host and a briefing on the contest rules.

Warmest holiday regards and blessings of the season.

Your hostess,
Jenny.

Joy glanced at her snowman watch. "We better hurry if we're going to make it to the meeting. Are you okay to move between the cars?" Maybe this trip was a mistake.

"Mo-om." Chantal rolled her eyes like a teenager. She never called Joy Mom, she always called her Mama, just as Joy called her mother Mama. She must be annoyed to use Mom instead.

"Well then, we should go." She studied the car list to figure out how many cars they had to pass through. They locked up and made their way forward.

"Ladies and gentlemen," a cheerful female voice boomed out of the intercom, "we'll be underway momentarily." As if on cue, the whistle blew, and the train gave the slightest lurch forward. Chantal cheered even as she wobbled.

"I'm so excited," she blurted. "Christmas on a train." Her laughter was contagious. "Can we read *The Polar Express* tonight?"

"Absolutely. I brought a different book for every night." Reading together was a nightly ritual and blessing.

"Yay!"

Yes, she'd dragged books along. Several for Chantal and her e-reader was loaded with a dozen Christmas romances from the library. She couldn't wait to dive into the one about being snowbound, though the thought of actually being trapped made her shudder.

The acceleration was slow and steady and, to Joy's surprise, her daughter didn't stumble once as they moved along, passing through accordion-fold links between cars. She couldn't help but notice some passengers moving ahead of them, and others staying seated in the elegant dining car. Not everyone on the train was involved in the competition, like the troglodyte who had snapped at her earlier. He'd flat out said he paid to be here.

Okay, Joy, let it go. He's in the past and you need to forgive and forget about his rudeness.

Joy's emotions roiled like a churning sea. First elation that she might win and become debt free, second that she might fail, or Chantal might get injured. She decided to take the advice she repeatedly gave her child, reached for optimism, and shifted her fears to the back of her mind.

They entered the forward observation car where people filled every seat with a few left standing near the back. The car was elegant with oak and mahogany accents and shining brass trim. It was decorated with evergreen and ribbon swags, bright fairy lights and shining glass balls. It smelled faintly of peppermint and cocoa.

Just inside the coach's door, a pretty blonde woman in scrubs stood beside an old man in the narrowest wheelchair Joy had ever seen. The man reminded her of Albert Einstein. It must be awful to maneuver a wheelchair on the train. *Were they contestants?*

At the far end, at the front of the car, a young woman dressed as Mrs. Claus stood behind a wooden podium. "Ah," she called. "Here they are, our final contestants."

Every head in the room turned toward them, and Joy wanted to slink into a corner for being late. She hated being in the spotlight.

She was a complete and total introvert unless she was behind her desk at work or protecting her daughter.

"Here, take my seat."

Joy turned toward the voice. The man who had stuck his nose into her argument stood and gestured to his chair.

"Go ahead, Chantal," she said. Chantal wasn't weak, but the short walk on a moving train hadn't been the easiest for her. "Thank you, sir," Joy said.

"Seth. Seth Mathison." He raised one eyebrow as if waiting for Joy to provide her name. When she didn't, he stepped aside so Chantal could sit. Joy leaned against the back wall and glanced out at the city slowly passing by through the enormous arched windows of the observation car. She couldn't wait to be staring out at snow-covered mountains. She'd never seen snow before they arrived in Denver yesterday. The sight still thrilled her. Even the dirty, slushy city snow.

Seth leaned beside her. Not too close, but close enough she could just get a hint of his minty fresh breath and light spicy aftershave. She peeked at him from the corner of her eye. He was clean-shaven and wore jeans and a simple navy hoodie with a tiny logo she didn't recognize. He looked casual and comfortable. Not like many of the others who seemed either excited or tense.

He nudged her and nodded to the front of the room. She realized that while she was gawking, their hostess had begun her talk.

"Welcome, everyone. I'm Jenny. I'll be your hostess for this trip. If you need anything, look for me, or for one of our service staff members. You'll recognize them by the lapel pins they wear." She held up a shining pin. Even from the back, Joy recognized it as the train company's logo.

Jenny went over some housekeeping details and meal schedules. "Our dining rooms are large, but not enormous. You'll be given a schedule of your assigned mealtimes. There are always snacks in the lounge car, and you can request food at any time. Remember, this is an all-expense paid trip for the contest participants." She paused. "And for the family members that accompany them."

There were only four other children that Joy could see. Two looked to be about twelve, and two were toddlers. Nobody close to Chantal's age. Maybe there were other children onboard who weren't involved in the contest. She sighed. It would be okay; this was the perfect time to bond with her daughter, and their information package had mentioned daily activities.

"Now, onto the contest." Jenny rubbed her hands together and grinned. "This is going to be so much fun." She looked around the car. "As you know, first prize is twenty-five thousand American dollars. Second prize is ten thousand. The funds will be donated to the winner's pre-approved charity."

Since Joy's application had been accepted, she assumed that paying off her daughter's medical bills met the contest's criteria. She closed her eyes and sent a silent prayer to God, and to the Spirit of Christmas, that she'd have what it took to win. Working two jobs was taking away from her family time, and lord knows she'd love an evening all to herself with no other commitments.

"As you know, you'll be assigned a task to complete during the course of the journey." Everyone nodded. "What you might not know is that you'll complete your task with a partner. Everyone has been paired up by our benefactor."

"Who is the benefactor?" someone up front called out.

"Can we choose our own partner?" A deep male voice asked.

"Our benefactor wishes to remain anonymous." Jenny adjusted her wire-rimmed glasses. "You will work with the person you are assigned. Failure to do so will result in disqualification."

"I hope I'm paired up with someone good." Seth's whisper danced along Joy's nerves. He had the greatest voice. Deep and husky, it did something delicious to her insides and set off a chain of longing that she hadn't felt for years.

"Me too," she whispered back, silently hoping to be paired with someone who wouldn't have an issue with her daughter's limitations.

Joy raised her hand.

"Yes, there in the back?" Jenny peered over her round gold-rimmed glasses.

"What if you don't have the same charity?"

"We'll discuss that problem if it crops up for the winners."

"Will we be paired with someone with the same charity?" Joy asked nervously. She needed this money so danged badly.

"Not necessarily. Our benefactor has done the pairing. There will be no disputing your partner. Remember, this is about charity. It's about fun. It's about the magic of Christmas, and the fullest enjoyment of all the season offers." Jenny went over a few more rules, all of which had been outlined on the contest's entry form.

"As you can see," she waved toward the window. Across a snow-covered field, brilliant white-capped mountains seemed to glow in the sunshine. "We've passed out of Denver. Please enjoy the scenery and take advantage of the many offerings on our train. Get to know your fellow passengers. This is a wonderful time to make new friends. You will be notified of who you are paired up with shortly."

"Wow," Seth said. "That left as many questions as answers."

"I wonder how they plan to pair us up. I wonder what the tasks are," Joy mused.

"And when we'll know who our partner is. What's your charity?" Seth asked.

Heat flooded Joy's face. She hated to admit that she was the charity. "The Cerebral Palsy Association." A partial truth. They'd get what was left over after she paid the medical bills. "You?"

"The Alberta Children's Hospital's burn unit." His brows pinched together, and the corners of his lips turned down.

"That's a great charity. Nice choice. Does it have special meaning for you?" she asked as people filed out past them.

"I'd rather not discuss it. Have a wonderful trip." He nodded briskly and walked away. He took a seat near the front of the car and stared out the window.

She snorted in disgust. What was with him? She reviewed their brief conversation. The burn unit kept repeating in her mind. He must have lost someone. How tragic was that? Compassion flooded her heart. Seth Mathison was a man who needed a bit of care, and she hoped he found it. And she hoped he wasn't her partner for the contest.

Chapter Three

Seth ignored the bright Christmas decorations precisely placed around the observation car and stared out the window at the snowy fields passing by. He'd never been to Denver. This was his first trip to the U.S. that didn't involve Texas or Florida. The landscape here was so much like Calgary, it almost made him homesick. He chuckled at the idea. He'd only left home yesterday. How could he miss it already?

"Can I sit here?"

He turned to his left. The girl with the walking sticks, Chantal, stood there looking at him as she swayed with the train's motion. Her smile was wide, her eyes bright and eager. She pointed at the two-seater mini sofa facing him. The seats in the observation car were small but extremely comfortable.

"Sure. It's a public train." He didn't mean to be grumpy, but the girl's mother's question about his charity had brought a fresh rush of pain over the memory of his niece's death. She'd died in an arson fire five years ago and his whole family still ached with the loss.

Chantal confidently maneuvered to the seat and sat down, propping the sticks between the sofa and the wall. She gave him a knowing look. "You didn't really mean it was okay to sit here," she said wisely. "It's okay. I'm used to people being weird about me. Mama says that's their problem, not mine."

"Chantal," her mom's voice came from behind him. "Don't be rude."

"You do say that," the girl frowned.

"Yes, but some conversations aren't meant to be shared." She walked to the end of the sofas. "Come on now, leave Mr. Mathison alone."

"Call me Seth. And you don't need to leave. Please sit." Chantal was just about the same age as his niece was when she died. Gwyn would have liked the outspoken girl.

Chantal's mom perched on the edge of her seat and looked out the window. She was quite pretty with her straight blonde hair and pretty deep green eyes. They reminded him of the moss on the trees in the provincial park his house in Calgary backed onto. She seemed nervous, like she didn't want to leave her daughter alone with him, but didn't want to be there either.

"What are your crutches called?" he asked Chantal.

"Forearm crutches. They're for cerebral palsy. They help me walk," she said, as if he wasn't smart enough to figure it out.

"I see that. You climbed the tall train steps very well. I was impressed." He had no idea what to say next.

"Look," Chantal screamed excitedly and pointed out the window.

The train was chugging slowly past a rocky wall where four Rocky Mountain bighorn sheep climbed like they were on flat land. "Their horns are huge," Joy said.

"I read that they are the state animal of Colorado and that the males' horns are curved," Seth told Chantal. They watched the group until they were out of sight. The excitement of the moment faded, but it had broken the discomfort between them. They chatted quietly about the contest and voiced their questions and concerns to each other.

Seth looked at the woman sitting across from him. They'd be on this train for the better part of December, which was a lot of time to spend together without knowing her name. This trip was a slow journey from Denver, Colorado, to Rocky Mountain House, Alberta. With stops almost every day.

"I'm Seth," he reminded her. "What shall I call you?"

"Joy. My name is Joy." She sighed as if she didn't want to tell him.

"Nice to meet you, Joy."

She didn't respond with the usual *nice to meet you too*. Instead, she said, "I do wish I knew who I was partnered with and how the tasks are going to happen."

"I'm sure we'll find out soon enough. It's a twenty-four-day trip and a hundred contestants are being paired up. That's at least two pairings every day. Some must happen on the train and I'm guessing some will happen at the stops," he said.

"I wonder what the first stop is," Chantal asked.

Seth chuckled when Joy frowned and said, "We've only been moving for twenty minutes, and you want to stop." She shook her head in that way all mothers seemed to master.

"You said we would see new places and play in the snow. I didn't get to try my new mittens yet," she said logically.

"On my way to the meeting, I overheard some staff talking about a bonfire. I haven't been to a bonfire in years," Seth said.

Joy winced when Chantal clapped her hands in excitement.

"I don't know. It'll be slippery outside, and a fire can be dangerous."

As much as Seth was a firefighter, he didn't think a bonfire was a problem if everyone was careful. Fire safety was critical, but living in fear of fire wasn't good. "Maybe we can figure out a way to take Chantal and keep her safe."

Joy's glare was like a kick to the solar plexus.

"If it's okay with your mom," he added, trying to placate Joy.

"We'll discuss it later. Time to go Chantal. I'll be right behind you. Don't leave this car without me," she warned, her voice vibrating with tension. When Chantal was a few steps away, Joy leaned close to Seth. "Do not interfere with my child. You know nothing about her illness or her capabilities. Mind your own business and don't make promises I can't keep."

The venom in her voice was astounding. A lesser man would be completely cowed by her mama bear attitude. But heaven help him. All he could think about was how incredibly sexy she was in her defense. Lucky for him, he knew better than to mention it. He'd learned a thing or two about dealing with women from his sisters. They claimed he was almost civilized now.

He nodded his acquiescence. "Joy, I'm sorry. I'll check with you before I suggest or offer anything. However, I am a firefighter, and I know how to keep a child safe during a bonfire. If you'd like, I'd be happy to escort you and Chantal to the fire. I could help ensure her safety." He wasn't certain why it was suddenly so important that Chantal see the bonfire, but he really wanted to take her.

Joy's cheeks flushed. "No. Thank you." The words were bit out. Her cheek muscles flexed like she was gritting her teeth.

"If you change your mind, I'm in car eighteen, room D. Stop by and let me know." He flashed his most trustworthy smile. "Or send me a message." He resisted offering his phone number because she did not appear to be interested in him, despite his interest in her. They could exchange numbers later.

Once Joy and Chantal left, he enjoyed watching the wintery farms and forests rushing past the window. Even during the day, many of the farms were lit for the holidays. *I'll be Home for Christmas* started playing in his head. This might just be the best Christmas ever.

A young man dressed in an elf costume came by with a tray of drinks. "Hi, I'm Cliff, part of the Rocky Mountain Christmas Train's holiday staff. Can I interest you in a cocoa or hot cranberry apple cider?" He held the tray in one hand and used the other to straighten his pointy-eared cap atop his tousled red hair.

"You know what? I'd love a cocoa, please."

He sipped the drink and, content to be an observer for now, watched a few passengers getting to know each other. He headed back to his room after placing the empty snowman mug on the bar. Back in his room, he kicked off his shoes and lay down on his bed. Something crinkled, and he got up again.

A cream envelope, identical to the one that had invited him to the first meeting, lay on top of his pillow. How had he missed that?

Dear Seth:

You'll begin your adventure tomorrow at 9:15 a.m. Come to the forward observation car to learn who your challenge partner is. Good luck.

Warmest holiday regards and blessings of the season.

Your hostess,
Jenny.

"And so it begins," he said with a laugh. He studied the map of the train he'd found on the dresser earlier. He took note of the cars he wanted to check out. The Banff Dining Car was three cars closer to the end of the train. And of course, the forward observation car was near the front of the train.

Rocky Mountain
Christmas Train

Chapter Four

T he train stopped for the night on a siding outside a small town
whose name Joy had already forgotten. They would travel by
day and stop at night, sometimes spending up to four days in one
place while challenges were completed.

Joy had always been a light sleeper in case Chantal needed her, so
it was no surprise that she awoke early the next morning to the soft
sound of someone in the hallway. It was still fully dark outside. Who

would be up and about that early? She crept to the door, careful not to wake Chantal who had been too excited to fall asleep the night before. She peered through the peephole. Nobody out there.

She opened the door and looked up and down the hallway. Still nobody. How was that possible? Nobody disappeared that quickly. As she eased the door shut, she noticed a cream envelope with her name on it on the carpet. Warily, she picked it up. Who would leave her a note? Sleepily, she stared at it.

"What is it, Mama?"

"An envelope." It was the same paper as their invitation to yesterday's meeting. She turned it over and slid her finger under the flap. The cream paper inside was decorated with a Christmassy train scene across the bottom. The top was a notification that they would begin their challenge tomorrow. Make that today. It was early, but it was morning. "We're up first for the challenge."

Chantal clapped her hands and giggled. "I'm so excited." Her eyes went wide, and she looked panicked. "Oh. I have to go to the washroom."

Joy hurried over and scooped her up. Rarely did Chantal mention her needs. That she did so, meant she was desperate. Joy had done her best to instill confidence and independence in Chantal. Her daughter was small, but still heavy enough to be awkward. She settled her in the washroom, set her crutches inside, closed the door, and climbed back into bed, though she knew she'd never fall back to sleep.

This was the moment she'd been waiting for. She couldn't decide what could have been worse, waiting days or maybe weeks to be chosen, or trying now and failing. "We won't fail," she vowed quietly. "We'll meet the challenge." *They had to! Her peace of mind and pocketbook were depending on it.*

She wasn't expecting to fall asleep, but her alarm woke her at seven-thirty. They had just enough time to prep for the day and eat before the meeting. Funny, she hadn't expected this trip to be so scheduled. She laughed at her naivete. Of course, it would be. There were one hundred entrants, which meant fifty challenges, to coordinate.

The meeting was, once again, in the forward observation car. She dreaded having to go to one in the rear observation car. Getting to the back of the train would be exhausting for Chantal. They made their way slowly forward, stepping aside for those faster and those going in the opposite direction. They took seats near Jenny's podium, and a worker in an elf costume offered them hot drinks and gingersnaps.

Judging by the lack of empty seating, it looked like almost everyone came out to hear about the challenges. The first pairing was two women. Blending their first names, Devin and Bev, created Team Bevin. They had to work alongside the local fire department to gather toys for their annual Christmas food and toy drive. Team Rancy, Randy, and Nancy's task was to convince one hundred people at their next stop to donate money or books to the local library. They had to do this in a coffee shop and had only four hours to meet their total. Neither of these tasks seemed too difficult.

"Next up is Joy Spencer and Seth Mathison. Stand up so everyone can see you." Joy and Chantal stood. Seth was near the back. He gave a little wave and sat back down.

"Your team's name is Team Triple Threat, because your daughter is the third member. Your task is a bit more complicated, but easily achievable," Jenny warned them. She grinned, and the crowd chuckled. "You'll be taking over a youth choir's concert in Lyons. Both their leaders are down with the flu. Seth, you're charged with keeping track of thirty-two children and seeing that they do their part. Joy, you'll be the emcee for the event."

Bile rose in Joy's throat. She hated public speaking. She was terrible at it. There was no way she could do this. She'd failed before they even started.

"Can we change roles?" Seth asked from the back. "Kids aren't my strong suit."

Joy perked up. It was a great idea.

"No, you cannot." Jenny frowned. "You will be supervised during your task." She paused. "Switching roles will result in immediate expulsion from the contest, and you will be asked to leave the train." She looked the crowd over. "Cheating gets you kicked off the train. One more thing, Seth and Joy, we'll be stopping in Boulder. While we are stopped, you will need to find choir robes for your troupe. Or some other sort of cohesive outfits. You'll be given a list of sizes. What you choose is up to you, as long as you are within your allotted budget."

Joy groaned. She was not a shopper, especially when she didn't know what she wanted, or where she was going, and had to drag Chantal along. *And why was their task so much more complicated than the others?*

"How do we travel within town?" Seth piped in with Joy's thoughts.

"You'll be met by a volunteer. The vehicle will be easily accessible for Chantal."

"Wait! The kid is coming with us?" He sounded indignant.

"What does that mean?" Joy stood and whirled to face him. "Of course she's coming. Did you think I'd just abandon my child on the train?" The man was a colossal jerk.

His face went red, and his brows pinched together. "No. I was just surprised."

Joy snorted. *Why did she get stuck with him?*

"You'll be given a list of the songs they are performing," Jenny spoke into the middle of their disagreement. "Be sure you know the words. You'll have three hours in Boulder to buy what you need, then the train rolls out. We'll be stopping at a farm outside of town for the bonfire you've all been hearing about. It's part of the town Christmas Fair. We hope you'll take part while we're there."

Joy loved the stop they'd made yesterday. They had visited a Christmas tree farm/petting zoo where she had bought a tiny stuffed reindeer for Chantal. They were going to place it on the table in their room. Chantal loved the reindeer, but she went crazy for the make-your-own hot chocolate station. *How would she convince her daughter that they didn't want to go to the bonfire?*

"The rest of you can visit Boulder while we are stopped. We won't hold the train if you are late. We'll arrive in Boulder in twenty minutes. Please register with the staff before you leave the train. There is a list of attractions for every stop in a folder in your room. Are there questions?"

A flurry of questions erupted, though Joy was only dimly aware of them. How was she supposed to work with a man who didn't want to be around her daughter? The very idea was ludicrous. He said he wasn't good with kids, yet he'd managed to talk to Chantal yesterday without trouble. Chantal had spent half an hour last night talking about how nice he was and how he didn't treat her like a kid or a cripple.

Joy hated that word. Cripple. So derogatory and demeaning. Her daughter was a child with a disability. Although she wasn't that either. She faced mobility challenges and dealt with them very well. Her upbeat attitude constantly surprised Joy.

Rocky Mountain
Christmas Train

Chapter Five

S eth waited for the crowd to disperse before leaving the train. A twenty-something man stood on the platform holding a sign with their names. Joy and Chantal were making their way toward him. He watched Chantal move; she didn't seem to have any difficulty with her crutches, though there were a couple of icy patches on the platform. He gave them a moment to reach their driver before striding forward to join them. He didn't want them to feel rushed.

They had plenty of time to do their shopping. At least he hoped they did.

The dull winter sun made Joy's hair shine like gold. She wore a stylish, but well-loved, red wool jacket. The black and gold scarf draped around her neck glittered in the dim sunlight. She looked happy, but nervous.

He echoed those emotions. He was worried about failing. The burn unit needed this money. With the winners being broadcast on both Canadian and American television and widely on social media, the publicity would be enormous. He'd get a chance to talk about fire prevention and safety too, thus raising awareness.

"Are you Seth?" the dark-haired man asked.

"I am."

"I'm Adesh. I'll be your driver. The car is just over here." He pointed and led them through the thinning crowd. "Where to?" he asked once they were all piled into the back seat.

They hadn't had any time before now to come up with a plan. "Can we have a few minutes to decide?" Seth scratched his ear. He turned to Joy. "Any thoughts on how to create a coordinated look? Do we want actual choir robes, or something else?"

"I was thinking black pants for the boys, skirts for the girls, and a brightly colored top. Maybe rich green or red?"

"If they all had button shirts, they could wear matching ties," Chantal said. "Or white shirts and bright ties."

"Interesting idea. I like the idea of choir robes, myself." He watched his partners to see what their honest opinion was. Chantal frowned; Joy looked thoughtful. "Jenny did specify choir robes," he reminded them.

"She also said some other sort of cohesive outfits. I think the pants idea would work." Joy snapped her seatbelt closed and watched her daughter do the same.

"Hm. I still prefer robes. It is a children's choir. Let me do a quick internet search and see if I can find robes." After five minutes, he came up dry. Only one shop carried choir robes, and their lead time was too long.

"I guess matching outfits is the solution," Joy said. "I'm not sure how to do it. Retail probably won't work. We'd have to hit dozens of stores to find everything and might fail in the end."

The worry in her voice bothered him. They both wanted this badly. He didn't like the idea of potentially sharing the prize money. He'd rather have it all. But since he didn't want to lose, he searched frantically for a solution.

"Mama, I'm hungry. Can we think and get something to eat at the same time?"

Seth laughed. "I could use coffee. Maybe we could hit a drive-through. If it's okay with you, Joy."

"We really should get started." Joy's frown sucked all the good vibes from the car.

"If I may," Adesh said. "There's a small coffee shop about five blocks down and probably not out of our way if we're searching for garments. It isn't a drive-through, but they have the best coffee and treats." He smiled at them in the rearview mirror.

"Fine." Her frown said it was anything but fine. "Take us there."

Seth hid his grin and started searching for clothing companies in Boulder. By the time they reached The Coffee Loft, he had narrowed the possibility to two manufacturers. One was close, only about twenty minutes. The other was almost an hour away. That meant they'd be pushing their time limit. He explained the situation as they waited their turn in line.

"I say go to the closest one. We can't risk being late getting back to the train. We'll fail if we don't make it back in time."

"Or we could split up." The idea made sense to Seth.

"I don't think we can. Besides, if we split up, how would we know what the other has chosen?"

"We could send pictures. I could take a cab to the far place." He really didn't want to mess this up by ending up without proper outfits for the kids. "Jenny didn't say we had to stay together."

"True. But do you want to separate and find out we were wrong? I can't take the risk of being accused of cheating and getting thrown off the train."

"No! I want to ride to Canada," Chantal blurted, grasping Seth's sleeve, and pulling on it. "Please, Mr. Mathison. Stay together. I want to see Canada." Her eyes shone with tears.

A little piece of the ice he'd protected his heart with since his niece's death melted. He could picture his niece begging to finish the trip. "We'll stay together." He tapped her on the nose. "Just for you, munchkin."

"Where do you want to start?" Joy smiled gratefully over Chantal's head.

"Let's get our order to go and hit the closest place." She agreed. With luck, this would be their last argument of the day.

Before he finished his coffee, they arrived at Galliger's Dress Works. Silly name for a clothing company, if you asked him. Though they must know what they were doing, the sign indicated they'd been in business since 1856.

He hopped out and tried to remain patient while Chantal fumbled her way out of the vehicle. He had to admire the strength in her arms as she lifted herself, scooted across the seat, and moved her legs one at a time. Joy held out her crutches, Chantal grabbed them and they hurried toward the warehouse entry.

"Are they open to the public?" Joy asked.

He gestured for her to go ahead of him up the narrow walk. "I don't know. Their website didn't say they weren't." He shrugged, even though she couldn't see it.

"Oh boy. Maybe we should have gone to the other place," she fretted.

He placed his hand on her shoulder, gently pulling her to a halt. She turned to look at him, questions in her eyes. "We're here now. I'm sure we'll find what we need. We can always hit a mega mall if we need to. If we rented a scooter for Chantal, we could shop an entire mall in no time flat. She opened her mouth, snapped it shut, and nodded.

"Here's hoping they'll let us in."

A receptionist greeted them with an unhappy look. "Sorry, we aren't open to the public."

Seth stepped forward and smiled. "We're on a mission of mercy," he explained their situation, hoping she'd like the smile his mother said was so amazing. Quickly, he laid out their mission.

"I'm sorry," she repeated. "We aren't open to the public. This isn't a retail shop."

"Thanks for your time." He turned to leave.

"Wait," another voice called. He turned toward the double doors behind the receptionist.

"You said you're with the Rocky Mountain Christmas Train?"

"Yes, we are," Joy said. Her voice rang with enthusiasm.

"My brother applied to be on the train, though he never got in. He did make the shortlist in case someone canceled. Apparently, nobody did."

"That's too bad," Seth said. "I heard there were thousands of applicants for the one hundred spots."

"What is your charity?"

"Mine is the Cerebral Palsy Foundation."

The woman smiled, obviously understanding why. "What's yours?" She nodded towards Seth.

"The Alberta Children's Hospital Burn Unit." He swallowed the lump that formed in his throat every time he thought about his niece.

"Wonderful charities." She turned to the receptionist. "Helen, why don't you take an early break? Be back in an hour. I'll help these lovely people out."

Helen sputtered for a moment, clearly not pleased to have her control usurped. The other woman stepped forward and offered her hand. "I'm Michaela Frost. Call me Mikki." After they all shook hands, including Chantal, she rubbed her hands briskly together. "Let's get this party started."

She flung open the double doors to the warehouse with a flourish. "Welcome to my domain. I'm going to recommend against a black-and-white color scheme," she said. "The choir will look like a private school. This is a Christmas concert. Let's liven it up with color."

"That's what I said," Chantal exclaimed.

"Right this way. I just received a shipment from our Canadian factory. It's the last of our Christmas jewel tones." She walked toward the back. Several workers nodded or smiled as they passed. A couple of people looked surprised to see them.

Mikki pulled out a rolling rack of hanging shirts. "Look at these beauties."

The rack was filled with boldly colored dress shirts. The rack beside it held matching blouses with small frills on the cuffs.

"Oh, they're pretty," Chantal exclaimed. "We need the bright pink and gold."

"The fuchsia is lovely, isn't it?" Mikki said. Seth admired the way she corrected the girl without seeming to.

"The boys would look good in the deep green and the royal blue," Joy suggested.

"What about red? It is a classic Christmas color," he said.

"You don't want to overwhelm the audience with too much. You need to limit it to four, maximum, or you'll lose the cohesiveness. I suggest red and gold for the boys. Silver and green for the girls. Those are the colors we have the most of. What sizes do you need?"

Seth handed over the list and Mikki called over one of her staff members. "Would you please pull shirts in these sizes? Try to keep the amount of each color even. Joy will help you while Chantal and Seth come with me to find pants and skirts."

"Oh, Chantal can stay with me," Joy said hurriedly, her worry clear.

"Mo-om," Chantal groaned. "I'll be fine with Mr. Mathison. I'll be good."

"I'll keep a close eye on her," Seth offered, a touch annoyed that Joy didn't trust him. She was very protective of Chantal, maybe over-protective.

Joy twisted her purse strap between her fingers. "Let me give you my phone number in case you need me," she said.

Seth barely resisted rolling his eyes. Instead, he handed her his phone. No sense fighting Mama Bear. He'd learned that from his sisters. "I swear that I'll watch her."

Mikki clapped her hands, eager to show off her wares. "This way." She walked at a speed that didn't seem to challenge Chantal.

"I hate when Mom does that," Chantal grumbled as soon as they were out of earshot.

"Does what?" Seth knew but wanted to hear it in the girl's words.

"Treats me like I'm stupid or an invalid. I've told her a billion times that invalid is spelled in valid. I am valid. I'm just..." she paused. "I'm different, but I'm capable too. I know what I can and can't do. She doesn't even like to let me try new things." Her voice quivered like she was on the verge of tears.

Mikki gave her a side glance but said nothing.

"She's worried," Seth offered, feeling out of his depth but somehow understanding all the same. "And she let you come with us. Baby steps, right?" He offered his fist, and she gave him a fist bump without wobbling.

"Here we are." Mikki stopped by a rack. "Oh, we'll need the list."

"I've got it on my phone. We have fifteen boys and seventeen girls. I'd like skirts for the girls and trousers for the boys."

They placed the clothing on a rolling rack as they found the correct sizes. Trousers in the right sizes weren't difficult, though they had to mix two styles of black pants. Close enough in Seth's mind. Matching knee-length skirts was harder. They came up short on three of the second-largest sizes.

Seth was starting to panic when Chantal said, "Do you have the next size up?"

"I do, why?"

"Mama can sew. Maybe she could fix them. You should call her Mr. Mathison."

He pulled out his phone and dialed. Joy answered before the first ring finished.

"What's wrong?" she shouted, panic in her voice. "What happened to Chantal?"

Whoa. Calling was a mistake!

"Joy, wait. She's fine."

"What? What's wrong, Seth?" He had to pull the phone away from his ear. She was shouting so loud he could hear her without the phone.

"Sorry. Chantal is fine. Nothing has happened."

"Give me the phone," Chantal said, wiggling her fingers for him to hand it over. He shrugged and passed it to her. She leaned her elbow on her crutch and held the phone to her ear.

"Mom. Mom! I'm fine. I just have a question." Seth could hear Joy talking, but couldn't make out the words. "Mom!" Chantal raised her voice. "I have a question. I'm fine." She listened for a second. "We can't find enough skirts unless you can make three smaller." She listened again. "K. Bye."

She handed the phone back to Seth. He put it up to his ear.

"Don't you ever scare me like that again, Seth Mathison. I nearly had a heart attack. I thought something had happened to Chantal. Never again."

"I am sorry. I didn't think it through."

"Obviously not. Get the skirts. I can alter them if they aren't enormously oversized. Did you get ties?"

"Neckties? No. Do we need ties?"

"I think the boys would look dapper with neckties."

Dapper? He rolled his eyes. "I'll check with Mikki and get back to you." He hung up as Mikki shook her head no. "We could probably do without them anyway."

"They would look good," she said. "Let me make a call." She talked and pushed the rack towards the lobby. Seth and Chantal followed.

"Mom was really mad, wasn't she?"

"Yup. But it's okay. I've been shouted at before." He winked at her. "My sisters shout at me all the time when I mess up." Well, one of them did. The other barely spoke since her daughter died. Therapy was helping, but her recovery was slow and painful. Even though he was a firefighter, and had experienced tragedy and loss, Seth had done therapy as well. The entire family had, but Chantal didn't need to hear about that.

Joy joined them on the way to the lobby and told them her helper had already taken her selections to the desk. Mikki entered their purchase into her computer. "I'm giving these to you at cost," she said and named a ridiculously low price.

"That's way below our budget. We were given funds to pay for this. You don't need to cut your profit out," Joy said.

"Tell you what, if the organizers agree, you can give the leftover funds to your charities and split it between them with my compliments."

"That's so generous," Joy said, her eyes tearing up.

"We'll make sure you get a receipt," Seth promised and slid her enough cash to cover the bill. "All we need now are the ties."

"My friend is having neckties for the boys and pendants for the girls delivered to the train. She runs an accessory shop. She's hooking you up for free. But if you happened to mention our businesses to others, that would be great." She gave them the name of her friend's shop.

"You can count on that," Seth promised.

Chapter Six

J oy couldn't believe their good fortune. "That was incredibly generous of Mikki," she said as they loaded garment bags into the car.

"It's Christmas, a time of hope and generosity," Seth reminded her.

"Christmas magic," Chantal exclaimed.

Joy couldn't help but share an amused glance with Seth. His lips turned up and his brown eyes sparkled. She realized, once again, that he was a very handsome man. Tall and broad-shouldered, he was exactly the type of man she'd go for, if she were looking. At the vet clinic where she worked, she was almost the same height as most of the men. Being five foot seven, she looked up at Seth; he had a good five inches on her, maybe more. She liked the feeling of looking up at him. Wait, she wasn't looking for a man. Not a temporary one, not a permanent one. At least not until Chantal was much older.

The moment of shared levity passed, and she climbed into the car. Seth waited until she was in, closed her door, and got in on the other side. Chivalrous too. He was racking up a lot of points. He needed to; after nearly causing her heart to explode when he called. *Men! They were adorable, but could be so thoughtless.*

"Wow," Seth said. "We have seventy-five minutes to spare. What should we do? Or would you prefer to go straight back?"

"Can we go to the mall?" Chantal asked. "I want a warmer hat. It's cold here."

Seth's deep chuckle sent shivers down Joy's spine.

"It's only twenty-three degrees Fahrenheit. That's minus five Celsius to those of us from Canada. That's barely cold at all."

"We're from California," Joy said. "Twenty-three degrees is dang cold for us." She couldn't help but shiver. The car was warm, but not warm enough to suit her. Seth had taken off his gloves and stuffed them into the pocket of his unbuttoned wool jacket.

"Can we? Can we go to the mall?"

Joy looked at Seth, who gave an infinitesimal nod. She nodded back. "Is there a mall that isn't out of the way?" She asked Adesh.

"About five minutes away. Did you want me to take you there?"

"Yes, please!" Chantal called.

Adesh met Joy's eyes in the rearview mirror. She nodded.

"Okay, it won't be long."

It was the first Saturday in December, and the mall lot was packed. Adesh dropped them off at the door and agreed to come back to pick them up in just under an hour.

Joy grimaced, and they made their way past a crowd lined up outside a coffee shop. This was a huge mistake. She hated shopping most days, and that dislike amped up during the Christmas rush. The mood was chaotic. People chatted and laughed. Many plodded ahead with grim determination, frowns marring their faces. Others wandered like they were in a flower garden enjoying the blooms. The only upside was the bright, cheerful holiday music playing. She loved Christmas music. Even secular stuff like Wham's *Last Christmas*, which was playing when they entered.

"What do you want to look at?" Seth asked as they stepped through the double doors.

Joy barely took her eyes off Chantal. She was terrified her daughter would be knocked over. Chantal named a popular outerwear shop. Two young boys raced past as Seth checked the mall map for the shop Chantal wanted. Their mother screeched at them to come back. Joy shuddered in fear.

"It's upstairs." He jabbed his thumb to the left. "We can take the elevator. Luckily, it isn't too far."

"There's a bench. Why don't you guys wait here, and I'll run up and get a hat?" She forced all her enthusiasm into the suggestion, hoping they'd think a rest was just what they needed.

"Mo-om. I want to choose my own. You'll pick something girly or for a little kid."

Joy clenched her fists and reminded herself that this train trip was their first vacation since Chantal's diagnosis just over four years ago. Her daughter deserved to enjoy herself.

"How about I walk just ahead of you?" Seth offered. "You know, break a trail through the crowd so it's easier to navigate."

Joy hated the idea, but if they were going to do this, it was probably their best plan. "I guess that works." She hated that her voice lacked any sort of enthusiasm. She probably sounded like she was headed for major surgery.

"Come on, Joy. It'll be fun. It's not far. We've got the time." He started forward. People stepped around him, leaving a space for her and Chantal to follow. He was like a boat, and they were traveling in his wake. It was easier going than she'd anticipated. Seth breaking trail was a good idea. They reached the elevator in no time and found there were fewer people on the second level, though the store itself was packed. She'd swear that half the people in the mall were enjoying the holiday atmosphere rather than shopping. She was looking through a pile of hats when Chantal tugged on her arm.

"Look, Mama. Isn't that the lady from the train? The nurse with the old man in the wheelchair?"

She glanced up. "It sure looks like her." She was with a tall, broad-shouldered man with thick brown hair. They seemed to be arguing about something. Idly, she wondered who was looking after the old man if his nurse was shopping.

"It does look like her," Seth said. "The man looks vaguely familiar, too. I wonder if he was on the train. It was so busy I didn't get a good look at everyone and didn't pay much attention to the passengers who weren't contestants."

She studied the pair through the passing crowd, trying to be discreet. "You're right. There is something about him that seems familiar." She shrugged. "Maybe he just has one of those faces." She had a cousin who was always mistaken for random other people. It happened.

"That lady is from the train too," Chantal pointed to a woman walking out of a store.

"Don't point, dear. It isn't polite." She was right, though; the second woman had been sitting near the back of the welcome meeting. She stopped to talk to the woman they thought was the nurse, confirming suspicions that she was, indeed, from the train. Maybe the man was too.

"Can we go to the food court? I'm starved," Chantal begged after they gathered their hat and mitten purchase.

"I don't think so," Joy said. She couldn't wait to get out of this mall. She twitched with tension and fear that Chantal would stumble in the jostling crowd.

"Why not?" Seth asked. "We've got time if the lines aren't too long. I could eat too. My coffee shop muffin is long gone."

"I'm worried about the crowds."

His brow wrinkled. "It's not that busy," he said. "Why don't we go and grab a snack before we go back?"

"I already texted Adesh. He'll be at the door by the time we get there. We're done here. We got what we came for." Chantal's hurt look cut her like a sword. Seth's incredulous look was almost as bad. For a moment, it looked like he'd argue. His brows furrowed, and he stuffed his hands in his pockets. His shoulders hunched together, and he shook his head.

Slowly, he turned and headed out of the store. He didn't say a word, but his entire body radiated disappointment. Or was it disapproval?

As they made their way toward the elevator, the lights flickered and went out. Someone screamed. Joy stepped forward and placed her hand on Chantal's shoulder. "Hold still until we know what's going on."

The emergency lights came on, giving the mall a dim glow. All around them, people stared in confusion.

"What do we do?" She asked Seth when he turned toward her.

"Let's stay calm." There was a reassuring evenness to his tone. "I studied the map earlier. There is an escalator just to our left. Let's head that way."

"It won't be working," she said, hating how scared she sounded.

"No, but it's just stairs. We can take them down and out to the car."

"Chantal isn't good on stairs. She's slow. Other people will be taking them too. What if she gets pushed or something?"

"That's not a problem. I'm a firefighter. I'm quite adept at carrying people down the stairs." He flashed a roguish grin that hit her right in the heart.

"We'll walk over, and I'll carry Chantal down."

"I don't know." He was strong enough, but she always found it hard to trust men after her ex abandoned them, and this was her daughter.

He leaned in close so only she could hear. His faint masculine smell had her inhaling deeply. "Listen. In about two minutes, when people realize that the lights are staying off, assuming they do stay off, people are going to start to panic. Right now, it's fun. We want to be out of here before the panic starts."

She reared back at the quiet vehemence in his tone.

"Trust me, Joy. Just this once."

"Okay, let's go. Chantal, follow Seth. He's getting us out of here."

Chantal giggled. "It's like a haunted house. Everyone looks funny in the dark."

Seth and Joy shared an amused look, and they started forward. "Stay close," Seth advised over his shoulder.

Joy snorted. As if she'd do otherwise.

People were streaming down the escalator. Seth stopped twenty feet away. "Chantal, I'm going to pick you up. When I do, give your crutches to your mom. I'll carry you down the escalator and your mom will bring your crutches. Okay?"

"Are you gonna carry me like a firefighter? Over your shoulder?" She asked, her eyes wide with excitement.

"Is that what you want?"

"Yes!"

"It's not comfortable," he warned.

"Please." She looked at him, then at her mother.

"What's safest?" Joy asked.

"Honestly, the firefighter's hold leaves me one arm free to hold the rail or to push aside obstacles." He paused. "I've carried out two hundred and fifty-pound men that way. Down a ladder. We'll be fine."

"Fine." Gosh, she was so nervous. So much could go wrong. She cast a prayer heavenward that they'd make it down safely. "Let's go." She held out her hands for the crutches.

Seth scooped up Chantal. She laughed louder than she'd laughed for months. "Here, Mama." She thrust her crutches out and Joy grabbed them.

"Excuse me," Seth exclaimed. Everyone turned in his direction. "Coming through. Make way."

The solid authority in his voice made her swoon a little. People parted and let them come through. Chantal raised her head and grinned. She was having the time of her life. Thank heaven for the resilience of kids.

Seth carried Chantal down the escalator, back down the mall, and outside. He set her down beside Adesh's car. He waited for Joy to catch up. "Your taxi, your highness." He bent low and opened the door without shifting her position. "Ready?"

When she agreed she was, he swung Chantal into his arms and slid her smoothly into the back seat.

"That was so much fun," Chantal exclaimed as they pulled away. At the parking lot exit, they had to wait while six fire trucks pulled in. Whatever put the lights out must be serious.

They met Jenny in the observation car as the train rolled forward. Jenny and a crowd of participants cheered their success in gathering the required outfits. Jenny shook their hands and said, "You've got less than two hours until we stop at Lyons. You'll go immediately to the school to meet the singers and conduct your practice. The concert is tomorrow night."

Chapter Seven

S eth sat beside the window at a table in the forward dining car, waiting for the server to bring his lunch. In retrospect, it was lucky they hadn't gone to the food court. He'd heard on the radio that the fire had ended up being a false alarm—someone had tampered with the power. He breathed easier, relieved that it wasn't something worse.

Snowy scenery raced by in the same way that his thoughts were going. He supposed that as fast as trains usually go, they weren't moving very quickly. He was seriously dreading being in charge of a bunch of kids. Kids were not his strong suit. They were his kryptonite. He was a firefighter. Public speaking was easy. He spent a lot of hours canvassing for fire safety. But kids? No way. When it was time for school visits, he made certain he was on days off. He avoided those gigs like a dieter avoids donuts.

The server, a young girl in her twenties, set his lunch in front of him and gave him a flirty smile. "If you need me, I'll be over there." She said as she pointed over her shoulder.

Holy smoking ashes. She was flirting with him. She was just a kid. "Thanks." He dug into his lunch without looking at her. Hopefully, she'd take the hint. The Denver sandwich was delicious. A bacon, onion, cheese, and green pepper omelet between toast. Add a coffee and a side of fries and he was in heaven. He was happy to eat because, by the looks of things, tonight would be a late dinner.

The car was nearly empty. Only the nurse and the older gentleman she cared for were there eating. They talked in low, subdued voices. It looked like they might be arguing. No doubt the old guy had definite opinions on his care.

The door between cars opened and Joy came in. She held the door open for Chantal. Chantal scanned the car, and her eyes lit up when she saw Seth just two tables away. She hurried toward him and dropped into the seat beside him.

"Hi, Mr. Mathison. I made you something."

"Oh?" He had no idea what to say beyond that.

"Mama, hurry up. I need my picture."

"Mind if we sit?" Joy smiled.

"Not at all, please join me."

"Mama!"

"Oh. Here you go." Joy handed Chantal a piece of folded paper from inside her cross-body purse.

"This is for you," Chantal wiggled in her seat like an excited puppy. She thrust the paper at him.

The outside of the paper said Mr. Mathison, in childish block printing. "Thank you." His nieces and nephew were often drawing pictures for him, and he made sure to respond kindly and enthusiastically despite his discomfort. Gently, he unfolded the lined paper, which had been torn from a notebook. Inside was a colorful picture of a firefighter carrying a girl down an escalator beside an enormous Christmas tree. It said, *Merry Christmas. Thanks for saving me. Love Chantal.*

Saving her? He hadn't saved anyone. All he'd done was carry her down a flight of stairs.

"I love it, Chantal. Thank you. I'm not sure I saved you, but the drawing is very nice. I like how you colored my uniform, and the girl looks just like you."

"You did save me." She clutched his arm. "I didn't want to freeze in the mall. It was dark and scary. And then there were all those fire trucks." Her eyes widened at the thrill of a near-miss tragedy. She shifted her crutches aside and dove under his arm and onto his lap to wrap her arms around his neck. "I love you, Mr. Mathison."

"I love you too." How could he not adore this girl? She was sunshine itself, courageous and generous. Her gratitude warmed his heart, maybe even melting a bit more of the ice around it. He blinked moisture from his eyes. *No way. He wasn't going to cry because of a hug and a picture. No way!*

He looked up at Joy, who shrugged as if to say, "What can you do with kids?" He grinned.

"Okay, Chantal, leave Mr. Mathison alone now. Let's go find a table and get something to eat."

"You don't have to leave. Stay and eat with me." Surprisingly, he meant the hastily offered invitation. Joy looked like she might object, but the server arrived with menus.

Lunch passed in a blur of sharing bad jokes and puns with Chantal. She was quick-witted and loved to joke. After they finished eating, he carefully folded his new picture and placed it in his wallet with a promise to display it on his fridge. Now, long before he was mentally ready, they were in Lyons at the middle school, where the concert would take place.

A tall, slender woman with kinky black hair met them in the foyer where they shared introductions. "I'm Ngozi Williams." She pronounced it as ng-GOH-zi. She explained that a local choir was performing the concert, not at all connected to the school. They had rented the gym space to accommodate friends, family, and the community. She followed up by saying, "The children are in the gym. Follow me."

Inside the gym, chaos reigned. Children laughed and screamed excitedly and raced around. Ngozi put her fingers to her lips and let out an ear-piercing whistle. Every child stopped dead and then raced over to them. Two teenage girls lagged behind the rest, clearly uninterested in what was happening and there under duress.

Ngozi introduced them and said, "I'll be in the staff room if you need me." She walked away, leaving thirty-two children, from six to sixteen, staring expectantly at them.

"Okay," Joy clapped her hands. "Let's set up for the first number and we'll get started. Let's do this thing."

The kids scattered, most of them climbing onto the stage at the front of the gym. Seth, Joy, and Chantal walked up the center aisle between rows of folding chairs.

"Chantal, why don't you sit over there? Seth, you can go on stage and keep an eye on things." She flipped open the script for the concert, moved onto the stage, and stood at the microphone placed staged right.

Seth did as he was told, but he didn't want to. He'd rather be the emcee. Several kids stood in the wide wing of the stage. A couple of boys were pushing and shoving each other back and forth. Seth made a psst sound and gave them a stern look. They fell silent, though the elbowing didn't entirely cease.

Joy said, "I'll read my introduction and then you'll start singing." She paused. "Do we have a conductor?"

"No," the group called in perfect chorus.

Not good, Seth thought.

"Mr. Algimony was doing it, but he's gone."

Joy's sigh was audible even without a microphone. "Is there anyone here who knows how to conduct?" When nobody answered, she asked if they usually had music.

"Mrs. Algimony plays the piano, we need music," one of the teen girls said, rolling her eyes.

"I guess all the piano lessons I took will finally pay off." Joy walked to the piano on the opposite side of the stage and sat. She flipped to the proper page in the music book, nodded to the kids, and started playing.

A few notes in, as one, the children opened their mouths and *Frosty the Snowman* burst forth. They weren't exactly in tune, and some voices were much louder than others, but they did well.

A young girl walked up to the microphone stand and pretended to use it. "I'm Amy. Our next song is *Oh, Holy Night*. She returned to her place in front of the risers the children shared. Joy flipped a page and started playing.

They ran through song after song. A few had to be repeated to get them right or to clarify lyrics. Overall, the kids were good sports, with only a little grumbling.

Occasionally, the children rotated positions on the stage. Some songs had actions led by different children. The actions for *Must Be Santa* had Seth stifling a laugh. So far, neither of the teen girls had taken part, nor had the two oldest boys. He wondered if they were pranking him and Joy, or if their part came later. After five songs, he walked out on stage.

"Okay, we seem to have a couple of non-participants. Someone want to tell me what's going on?" He looked from child to child. If something was up, someone would crack.

A small brunette girl in the front row cast the older kids a nervous glance and raised her hand.

"Yes. What's your name?"

"Wendy." She stared at her toes.

"Go ahead, Wendy," he urged. Joy walked to his side.

"Those kids are supposed to be singing too," she whispered.

"Shut it," the oldest boy snapped. "We don't want to sing stupid songs."

Seth waited a moment, hoping Joy would step in. He cast her a glance, and she looked away. She was taking their roles seriously. He didn't want to admit that she was right to do so. He hated dealing with kids. Especially teens with attitude. This was way out of his league.

"Come out here," he said. He gave the uncooperative kids 'the look'. They trudged forward, shuffling their feet. "So, you don't want to sing?"

Nobody responded. *Okay, Seth. You're a firefighter. You control things at work all the time. What are a few kids compared to a house fire?* He turned to Joy. "Why don't we take a break?" He had no idea what he was going to say to these kids, but he knew he needed backup. Joy nodded.

"Okay, everyone. Take five minutes. Go and get a drink. Don't be long." The recalcitrant four started to leave. "Except you four," he added. "Take a seat on the risers. With rebellious expressions, they trudged over and flopped down.

He didn't want to tower over them by standing; he was a big man. Instead, he pulled over the piano stool and sat. He looked at them, one after the other, and tried to come up with something inspirational to say. *Man, he sucked at this.* Joy sat just to the left of the girls and gave him a discreet thumbs up. He cleared his throat.

"I'm only here because my dad says I have to be," one girl blurted.

"Okay. I understand that."

"Me too," said the other girl.

Seth looked at the boys. Neither said a word. He expected that they were going along to impress the ladies. They looked to be about twelve, just coming to the age where they found girls and lost their minds. "What about you two?" he probed.

"Just don't wanna sing."

"I see. Are you being forced to be here as well?" He didn't look at Joy, who was trying to hide a smirk. If he did, he'd start grinning and ruin his stern presence.

"Um. No." The older of the two boys, who looked to be brothers, hung his head. "I like singing," he mumbled.

"Then why aren't you participating?"

The youth turned bright red.

"Son," Seth said and waited for him to look up. "I was a teenager once, too. A hundred years ago. I know what you're thinking. Trust me when I say you don't want to mess things up with your family for a girl. Do you enjoy singing? Sing. The whole girl thing will work itself out in time."

The boys nodded in unison.

He looked at the girls again. "I've had to do things I didn't want to do. You'll find time goes faster when you take part than when you sulk on the sidelines. If you don't want to be here, have an honest discussion with your parents. Explain how you feel. Maybe they'll listen." He stood and brushed his hands together. "Now, shall we sing?" He didn't let them refuse. With a bit of work, he corralled everyone back on stage.

Three more songs, and they were finished, except for the final two numbers.

"We can't do the next one," Amy piped up.

"Why not?" Seth asked.

"Because Evangeline is supposed to be an angel and she's sick." Seth consulted his script for the umpteenth time. The next number was a short retelling of the nativity story.

"Is everyone else here?" he asked. A small group stepped forward. "Do you have costumes?" He prayed that they did because it was too late to find any.

"Yes," they chorused in harmony.

"Is Evangeline's costume here?"

Amy nodded.

"Can I see it?"

He studied the simple costume and tried to find a solution. They couldn't skip the nativity story. It was what Christmas was all about. He needed a miracle.

"I could do it," Chantal offered. She was standing at the base of the steps.

"No, you cannot," Joy disagreed instantly. "Can one of you other children do this?" Nobody answered.

"Why don't we let Chantal do it, just for tonight, and we'll figure something out for tomorrow?" Seth suggested. "Maybe Evangeline will be back by then."

Joy frowned and glared. Chantal grinned.

"Please, Mama. Just one time."

Watching frustration and resignation move across Joy's face was almost comical, though Seth didn't understand why she was so reluctant to let Chantal help. The child had sat patiently through almost an hour of music and adjustments.

"What can it hurt?" Seth's question earned him a withering glare.

"Fine. Just today. Not tomorrow. Do you understand?"

"Yes, Mama."

Joy stomped down the stairs and helped Chantal up the six steps. Seth didn't blame her. There was no railing to grab if you wobbled.

"Let's go over this." Seth read the script aloud once. Luckily, Chantal only had a few lines. "Places, everyone."

The children on the risers sat. One of the chastised boys walked to the mic and began narrating the story. The players acted their parts and spoke their lines with almost no prompting. Chantal walked slowly across the stage and faced the seats. Her eyes lit with happiness. She started speaking the lines from *The Gospel of Luke* that Seth recognized from his youth Sunday school classes. "For unto you is born this day in the city of David a Savior, which is Christ the Lord..."

She must have already known the verse because she recited it without stumbling, her face glowing with pride. The scene wrapped up, Joy started playing, and the choir stood and launched into a rocking version of *Mary's Boy Child*. The song morphed into *We Wish You a Merry Christmas,* and they were finished. Joy returned to the mic and, in a shaking voice, gave the closing address just as parents started coming in.

Rocky Mountain
Christmas Train

Chapter Eight

W hen the last child had finally left with a parent, Joy rushed to Chantal. "You were wonderful," she praised. "But you are not going on stage tomorrow night." Her daughter's face went from blissful to angry instantly. Chantal turned and stomped over to where Seth was sitting in the front row, her crutches slamming into the floor with each step. She couldn't remember the last time Chantal had been that angry. Her daughter was very even-tempered.

Closing her eyes, Joy struggled not to be angry at Seth. This was his fault. He let Chantal do this. Now she was going to start thinking she could do many things far beyond her abilities. She was going to get hurt. Joy pushed her anger aside. Now wasn't the time.

"I'm going to practice my lines," Joy said.

"You should try them with the mic on," Seth suggested. "You mentioned that you're not good at public speaking. Trust me when I say the mic makes it worse."

Well, that was helpful. Not! She sighed. He had a point.

She walked to the mic stand and clicked the mic on. "Testing." Barely audible, her voice quivered. *Crud.* She cleared her throat and tried again. Louder, but no less shaky.

"Louder, Mama," Chantal said from the first row.

"Good evening." Panic hit her square in the chest. She sounded awful. Creaky and shrill. "I sound terrible." *She couldn't do this.*

Chantal laughed. "You sound like you, Mama."

Seth smirked.

He knew she'd sound this way. *Jerk.*

She tried again. "My name is Joy; I'll be your emcee for the evening." Her voice steadied, but still sounded wrong. So very wrong.

"Better," Seth said, taking a seat beside Chantal. "Pretend you're talking to us. Forget everyone else. It's just us."

She focused in on his face, and though he was six feet away, she'd almost swear she saw support there. She drew in a deep breath and began again. Her lines flowed and if she tuned out her own voice, she might get through this. Only Seth wouldn't be in the audience tomorrow. He'd be on stage. Closing her eyes, she tried to imagine she could get over her fears. Speaking up at staff meetings made her anxious. She'd never be able to get through this.

She practiced a few lines and flipped the mic off. Chantal and Seth cheered. She climbed down off the stage on wobbly legs. Seth rushed forward and offered his hand. Grateful, she took the offered support.

"Wow, that was terrible," she grumbled. Terrible didn't even cut it.

"Actually, that was pretty good. You'll be great tomorrow."

Chantal hurried over. "You were great."

She highly doubted that, but she'd accept the praise. "I guess we managed today." She grinned. They'd done it. One day down, and one to go. "Let's head back to the train."

Ngozi rose from a chair in the back of the gym and pocketed her cell phone. "All finished?" she asked as they walked toward her.

"Is there a good place to get dinner nearby?" Seth asked. "All those kids made me hungry."

Ngozi laughed. "There's a pizza place eight blocks west. I'd give them a try. They make terrific pizza and the best minestrone." She gave them directions.

"Shall we go to dinner, ladies?" Seth asked. "We don't have to worry about getting back. The train isn't going anywhere."

"There's going to be a huge bonfire in the park tomorrow night. You'll have a blast. There will be crafters and food trucks. It's the annual tree lighting party and Lyons Christmas Market."

"That sounds gre...," Seth said.

"I don't think so," Joy said, speaking over Seth.

"I want to go to the bonfire. Please, Mama. I've never been to one. All my friends have gone to bonfires." She drew the words out into the whine Joy detested.

"I don't think so. Let's just get some dinner and go back to the train. I'm exhausted. We can talk about this tomorrow." She didn't need this fight right now. Her stomach was already whirling with stress. She didn't know if eating would make it better or worse.

Chantal gave her the death stare. The one that said this wasn't over.

"O-kay," Seth dragged the word out. "Let's eat. I'm starved."

Fifteen minutes later they were led to a booth in the busy restaurant.

"Sit with me, Mr. Mathison." His eyebrows jerked up in surprise, but he climbed in beside Chantal who was pointedly not looking at Joy.

Great, she was going to pout all night. A tiny part of her said she was being unreasonable, but she didn't want her daughter to be injured. Maybe she'd made a mistake in bringing Chantal along on this trip. Or maybe the trip itself was a huge mistake. She almost groaned aloud. She needed the money and if nothing else, having someone pay all her food for a month was a huge saving. Christmas this year was special. They would arrive at their destination on Christmas Eve and be hosted at a hotel until the twenty-sixth, when they'd begin their journey home. It was the trip of a lifetime, but it wasn't going to include a bonfire. They'd find other fun things to do.

Chantal pouted longer than normal. She was surly when she ordered until Seth gave her a side look. She immediately brightened her tone with the server. That was a look Joy would like to master. Instant compliance without a word.

Joy clenched her fists and relaxed them. Stress over tomorrow night was making her hyper-sensitive and jumpy.

"We have some free time tomorrow," she said. "What shall we do?"

"The mall's out. The bonfire is out. There's nothing left to do." Chantal's glare would cut glass.

"I'm sure there are plenty of things to do," Seth said. "We just have to put our minds together and figure it out."

Joy wanted to kiss him for his support, though she suspected he thought she was a helicopter parent, never letting her child out of her sight or into potential danger. She wasn't like that, was she?

Seth pulled out his phone. "Let's do a search and see what Lyons offers for entertainment." He typed and scrolled. Chantal leaned in to peer over his arm.

Funny how her daughter immediately trusted Seth. She was usually wary around men. Not that Joy spent much time around men outside of work. But Chantal had never had a male teacher. Both her physiotherapist and doctor were women. She'd never taken to anyone, male or female, as quickly as she had to Seth.

Not that Joy blamed her. He was attractive and helpful. A bit off-putting at first, but he seemed to be a great guy. And a firefighter too. Who didn't love a man in uniform? She slipped into a fantasy vision of Seth dressed for work. Whew! The man should be on a calendar. And for a man who said he didn't get along with kids, he was doing great so far. Both with Chantal and the choir. What made him think he couldn't deal with kids? He was fabulous. He'd even straightened out the older kids with nothing more than a few words.

Seth and Chantal shared a ham and pineapple pizza. Gross. She detested pineapple on pizza. Joy had the chicken Caesar salad. She'd give her left foot for a glass of wine, but it wasn't in the budget. Maybe she could swing it, but she wanted to pay down their medical debts as quickly as possible and her conscience wouldn't let her indulge in the pleasure. Thinking about it, she couldn't remember the last time she'd had wine that wasn't at a work function.

Shoving the complaint away, she took a minute to count her blessings. She had a lovely, healthy daughter. They were on the trip of a lifetime and in the company of a nice man. If they were lucky, she might win the funds to pay off her debts. Life wasn't so bad.

"Mo-om." Chantal's impatient tone said she'd spoken more than once.

"Yes?"

"Were you listening?" Chantal rolled her eyes, and Seth smirked.

"Sorry, I was thinking about...about your Christmas gift," she fibbed. Seth's smirk turned into a full-on grin.

"Hey, look at this." Seth handed her his phone. "There's a Christmas train. We could go for a ride."

"Yay," Chantal cheered.

"Oh, I don't think so," Joy said sadly. It was fifty dollars a ticket. No way she could afford that.

"It would be safe. It says you board and stay seated while the train travels a ninety-minute circuit through a Christmas village and lighted forest. You get cookies and hot cocoa. This sounds a bit like *The Polar Express*. It's a decent deal."

She gave him a look.

brows came together in question. Chantal glared at her.

"Look, Joy. I'd love to go on the train, but I really don't want to go alone. Will you and Chantal please be my guests and save me from the embarrassment of being a single man on a family train ride?"

She blinked. How had he fathomed her problem so quickly? She wanted to be angry at him for prying into her life, and for wedging himself in where he didn't belong. Somehow, the hope on her daughter's face had her accepting.

"You know what? I think I'd like that. What do you say, Chantal? Shall we ride the train with Mr. Mathison?"

Chantal flung her arms around Seth. "Yes, please."

Seth called ahead, booked tickets, and requested early boarding. They hurried to finish dinner and were off to the train.

Seth smiled at the sweet joy on Chantal's face. She wriggled in her seat as the hot chocolate cart came toward them down the train aisle.

"Can you send Mama the picture you took of me with the elf?" she asked.

"Sure thing." He pulled out his phone and sent Joy the photos taken in front of the trainyard's gates. The sign over their heads welcomed them to the Santa Express. One of mother and daughter, and the second of all three of them together that a staff member had taken.

"Can I see, Mama?" Chantal asked when Joy's phone chimed.

"Oh, look at us," Chantal smiled up at Seth. "We look like a real family."

Her words hit him like a blast of heat to the heart. If this kept up, he'd be having feelings again. He tried to shore up his softening defenses. "We sure do, kiddo."

"Chantal," Joy said with a clear warning in her voice.

"I know, Mama. He's not my dad. But I like Mr. Mathison. He's my friend."

"He's our friend." Joy smiled at him, and he suddenly didn't care about anything more than getting to know the beautiful woman sitting across from him.

The trip flew by. They rode through an old west town with every building lit up with lights. Antique-looking gas lamps lit the corners. Slowly, the train rolled into a forested area where every tree glowed with warm lights. Each tree was different. Where one tree was pure green and another blue, others were white or multicolored. They ranged in height and breadth.

Seth spent more time watching Joy and Chantal than the passing scenery. He snapped several pictures as they traveled.

The trip was over too quickly and as they disembarked behind everyone else, he knew a moment of sadness that the night and his time with them had ended. Deep inside, he hoped to spend more time with them after they completed their task for the contest.

Rocky Mountain
Christmas Train

Chapter Nine

S eth watched Joy pace back and forth behind the closed stage curtain. Her nerves both echoed and amplified his. Only a few children had arrived. So far, they were playing quietly with little pushing or shoving. The oldest four had yet to arrive, and he honestly wondered if they would. None had an irreplaceable role in the performance, which was a blessing, but he'd be disappointed if they gave up on what could be a real life-changing experience.

He'd loved choir as a youth, at least until that concert when his voice had cracked. Thinking about that day still mortified him. He shuddered just thinking of it. They'd sold seven hundred tickets, and he'd had a lead role. On stage in front of a packed house, he stepped up for his first solo, opened his mouth, and nothing came out. He'd tried again, and his voice rose above the hushed crowd. Beautiful and sweet, until it cracked. He bolted off stage and hid in the shadows behind the backdrops. His understudy, so to speak, took over the role, and the concert went on without him. It was the last time he sang in public.

Tonight, he was hoping, no, he was praying, for a Christmas miracle that this would go off without a hitch. Especially for Joy.

Joy hurried to his side. "There aren't any empty seats," she cried, her eyes wide and scared. "People are lined up along the walls." She grasped his arm like she was grabbing a lifeline. "I can't do this."

"Yes, you can." He placed his hand over hers. She was icy cold. "Listen to me, Joy." He paused until he had her attention. "I can tell that you're a competent woman. I know that you've done great things raising a child without a father. Having a daughter with cerebral palsy must be an even bigger challenge. You've dealt with all these kids and being thrust into playing the piano along with your emcee role. You're strong, and capable; you can do this. I believe in you." With each statement, her eyes widened. When he finished, her bruising grip on his arm slacked.

"Do you think so?" she pleaded for reassurance.

"I know so. You've got this, Joy." He shook off her grip and grabbed her shoulders. "The person running this contest, whoever that benefactor is, seems to know everything about us. They've given us hard tasks. Maybe not logistically difficult, but ones that are personal challenges. I think they're doing double duty and getting us to stretch our limits, and they're doing that for a reason. Something besides winning the big cash prize. This is your test."

"O o okay," her voice shook.

"You can do it, Mama," Chantal called from her seat in the wings. With more than a full audience of spots sold, she'd given up her seat to sit backstage.

"I'm in just as bad a spot. I'm dealing with kids, for Santa's sake. Spending time with my nieces and nephew is hard for me. My guts are rolling, but I'm going to do this. For myself, for the chance to win. Because if I do, it, if we do it, our charities stand to gain a lot."

The pinched expression on her face lightened, though her frown didn't disappear entirely. Slowly, she nodded and pushed out an exaggerated breath. "Thanks. That helps."

The timer on his watch chimed. He shut it off. He clapped three times, and the children turned to look at him. "Okay, guys and girls, it's ten minutes to showtime. Miss Joy and I know you can do this. The gym is full, but remember, these are your families and friends. You've practiced this for months. You showed us yesterday that you've got it down pat. This will be as easy as pie."

"I like pie," one boy piped up, and everyone laughed.

"There will be pie and cake, and other goodies after the concert. So, let's pull together and do this. Are you with me?"

"Yes." The positive reply was loud and eager.

"If you have to use the bathroom, do it now. Go in pairs and stay together." The bathrooms were right outside the stage door. He stationed himself near the door and kept track of who left and who came back.

His alarm chimed again with three minutes to curtain time. Everyone was back from the bathroom and in their coordinating outfits. As expected, three had needed to be altered. One of the parents took on the simple alterations, saving Joy from the difficulty of doing them by hand.

Seth urged everyone onto the risers, straightening their outfits and smoothing unruly hair as they climbed up. "You guys look amazing," he said. Joy added her agreement.

"But Becky, Amara, and those boys aren't here," Amy whined.

"That's okay," Seth reassured her. He looked at every child, smiling positively. "I hoped they'd come, but you can do this without them. Raise your hand if you know the Christmas story or can read it well enough to read to the audience." Half the kids raised their arms. "Okay, you, I'm sorry I forgot your name." He pointed to a young man with floppy hair.

"I'm Jed," the boy said. "I know the story by heart."

"Okay, if the others don't show, can I count on you to tell the story? You can take my script, just in case you need it."

The boy beamed proudly. "Yes, sir."

With that crisis averted, his watch beeped. *Showtime*!

"Okay, it's time. Settle down everyone. Are you ready?"

They all nodded. There was a thump and a rustling at the side of the stage near Chantal's chair. Startled, Seth whirled round.

The last four students had arrived and were tossing their jackets aside.

"Aw, I wanted to tell the story," Jed said.

"Go ahead," the original storyteller said.

"What if you did it together? Each could read a paragraph. Take turns," Seth suggested. He knew that it was important for them all to take part.

The boys looked at each other and nodded slowly.

"Perfect," Seth praised, keeping his relief at both the agreement and the late arrival to himself. "Okay, remember, no matter what, Miss Joy and I are proud of you. Okay, Joy, take it away."

After waiting a few seconds for her to reach the mic, he nodded to the stagehand and the curtain slowly pulled back.

Joy clenched her hands behind her back and addressed the crowd. This was brutal. She scanned the room, looking for a friendly face. Jenny sat right up front. Joy kept looking and recognized several people from the train. She focused on Jenny, who nodded slightly and smiled. That simple smile went a long way to calming Joy's jumping heart.

With her pulse thrumming in her ear like an out-of-sync metronome, she flipped on the mic, swallowed hard, and said, "Welcome to tonight's performance of the Lyons Youth Choir. The Lyons com-nunity..." Someone in the audience chuckled.

She closed her eyes and took a breath. "Sorry about that. The Lyons Community Choir and the food bank. Thank you for coming out tonight." Her mouth felt like it was filled with cotton. Her lips stuck to her teeth. She took a sip of her water.

"The Rocky Mountain Christmas Train is happy to help with this worthwhile event. I am your emcee, Joy Spencer. My assistant is Seth Mathison. We are partners in the train's challenge. We are team Triple Threat, so named because my daughter is part of our team." She gave a brief rundown on the train's first annual event and how it would benefit many charities. Following her script, though not word for word, she encouraged everyone to tune into social media to follow the contestants' progress.

"Now, for our first number." She turned off the mic and, knees shaking, made her way to the piano. Moving the four-legged stool back, she sat. This event had called for a fancy dress. Fortunately, she had brought a floor-length velvet dress for Christmas dinner. Unfortunately, it was now stuck under the piano stool. She shifted and managed to free her skirt.

After a glance at the youths, she played the opening chords to *Frosty the Snowman*. The first voices were quiet, too quiet. She steeled herself for disaster. Another voice joined. Then another. Finally, what sounded like the entire choir was singing. By the end of the first verse, the trembling left their voices, and they sang with abandon. They'd done it, they'd lost their nerves and found their joy. In her excitement, her fingers tripped over each other, but the slight stumble didn't deter the singers.

She paused a moment for applause, then launched into *Oh, Holy Night*. The choir sang with abandon. At one point, she thought she heard a giggle but ignored it rather than mess up her playing. She was years out of practice, but by all that was holy, she loved playing. She needed to do it more.

As she played the line, 'Fall on your knees,' she heard a thunk. The crowd roared with laughter. She risked a fast glance at the risers. Three of the boys in the front row were on their knees.

Her fingers stumbled again; she focused on finding her place. The choir sang, though their voices were light with unspent laughter. The crowd settled, and she risked a glance at the boys. They were back on their feet, acting like nothing had happened. Little stinkers.

Thoughtfully, someone had moved the mic closer to the piano. Following the song, she introduced Amy, who read a short Christmas poem. Hans read a short story, and they were back to singing.

Finally, they were at the nativity scene. Almost done, and she hadn't butchered anything too badly. She made the introduction, returned to her stool, and turned to face the stage to watch.

The play began with two boys reading the script as the cast acted it out. The audience was dead silent. She heard a familiar tapping sound and spun her head toward the wings. Chantal, dressed as an angel, halo and all, made her way toward center stage.

Joy's heart stopped. Her vision went blurry. *Dammit, Seth. Why did you do this? Why did you put my daughter in danger?* He was going to pay for this. She sucked in a breath and gripped her thighs to keep from running to Chantal's side. If she got hurt or embarrassed, she'd kill Seth.

Chantal reached center stage and shrugged apologetically at Joy. Her smile was a hundred miles wide. She'd never seen her daughter happier. She was glowing. In a high clear voice, she recited her simple lines. She stood straight and strong, grinning until the short skit was wrapped up. She walked off the stage. The entire crowd rose to their feet, giving the children a standing ovation.

Joy sat, stunned, until Seth cleared his throat. She turned and launched into the last two songs. Somehow, between her anger with Seth, and her delight at how Chantal had done, she wrapped up her comments and directed the families and guests to the school's food service classroom for snacks and beverages.

Chapter Ten

Seth braced himself for the storm that was coming. He'd seen the fury on Joy's face and had to admire her for not rushing to Chantal's side as she usually did. She'd kept her seat and let her daughter take a chance.

He waited with Chantal in the far corner of the enormous room, which featured four full kitchens.

"Mama's gonna be mad," she said, her tone totally matter of fact, and not particularly worried.

"Yup."

"What should I do?" A hint of nervousness crept into her tone.

Good question. "What do you think you should do?" he asked, trying to buy some time to figure out his explanation.

"I don't wanna apologize," she said. "I wanted to do it, and I did. I was good."

Seth laughed. "Yes, you were."

Jenny strode over to them. "Well done, Chantal. You were wonderful. You should be very proud of yourself. Seth, that was a brave and possibly stupid thing you did with Chantal. I hope Joy gets over it. I saw the anger on her face."

The man in the wheelchair rolled up, his nurse right behind him. "Well done," the old man wheezed. "I'm Chris Watson. This here's Maddie." He jabbed a thumb at the nurse.

Seth said, "Pleased to meet you both." He shook hands with Maddie, then with the old man who had a ridiculously firm grip for a guy his age. Likely from pushing his chair.

Chris turned his attention to Chantal, praising her performance. Seth talked with Maddie, discussing the show and the train trip.

"I'm really enjoying myself," she said. "I'm glad Chris hired me to be his caregiver." She leaned close. "He's quite the pip, this one." She laughed.

Seth glanced at the old man again. His clothing was neat, though not new, and his shoes were well worn. He must have owned them before he lost the use of his legs.

"How did you hurt yourself?" Chantal asked. The question almost echoed Seth's thoughts.

The old man laughed. "Old age, sweetheart. And a war injury. I was a soldier."

"Oh." The child clearly didn't know what to say.

"What regiment?" Seth asked. He had friends who had served.

Chris waved off the question and said, "Oh, look. Isn't that your mom? She doesn't look happy."

Joy stormed across the room, dodging people without taking her eyes off Seth. No chance of escaping. It was time to pay the piper.

She reached his side, grabbed his arm, and led him away from the small group. "If you ever usurp my authority again, you won't live to regret it."

"Okay. But take it out on me, not on Chantal. This was one hundred percent my idea."

She glared. He knew he should be cowed by her ire, but dang, she was adorable in her defense of her daughter. Another chip of ice fell off his heart. Not as big as the one that had clattered to the ground as he watched Chantal on stage. Both mother and daughter were magnificent.

"Fine. This is all you." She shook her finger in his face. She opened her mouth, snapped it shut, and finally said, "Ugh," and stomped off.

Seth breathed a sigh of relief, but he didn't think for a single moment that he'd heard the last of this. He rejoined the group in time to hear Joy praising Chantal's performance.

"I'm sorry I didn't listen, Mama. I just wanted this so much. Don't be mad at Mr. Mathison. It was my idea." She clasped her hands together and looked apologetic. "It was all my idea, not Mr. Mathison's."

Joy smiled at Chantal and glared at him. It didn't matter. He was happy to take the blame because it had been his idea. He'd have to talk to Chantal about little white lies.

"We should celebrate your success," Jenny said. "Why don't we all go to the park and check out the food trucks and the Lyons

Christmas Fair?" She turned to Chris and Maddie. "You should come too. It's warm tonight, and I know a lot of the other passengers are coming. We're making a public announcement of the groups who completed their challenges."

"Can we Mama? Please." Chantal gave her mother puppy dog eyes.

"I already said no." She sighed.

Seth felt bad for Chantal. She'd been amazing through shopping and the rehearsals. Unless he missed his guess, they didn't get to have much fun time. To his surprise, Chantal didn't complain. She just stood silently, her eyes moist.

Joy looked around the group. Seth followed her gaze. Nobody met her eyes, and he could tell they didn't like her answer. She must have realized it, too.

"Do you promise not to wander off and to listen to me? No mistakes. No pleading. No disobeying or making little deals with Mr. Mathison?"

Chantal frowned. Then nodded. "Yes, Mama. I'll be good."

They returned to the train for proper outerwear, and before he knew it, they were at the park.

The Christmas fair was set up in a large open area not far from the Santa Train on the outskirts of Lyons. Thousands of feet had packed down the snow. Brightly lit trees surrounded the entire clearing. Between the trees, food trucks were parked, and open for business.

The enticing aroma of fried foods and chocolate immediately tantalized Joy. Tonight was going to be murder on her waistline.

Jenny had given her a stack of gift certificates good for any of the food vendors. A roving band of carolers dressed in period costumes strolled the path, pausing here and there to serenade guests.

To their left was an area surrounded by a picket fence with the area inside divided into sections. In each section was an enormous pile of snow. The sign announced a snowman building competition. They watched for a few minutes and moved on.

They indulged in burgers and fries and ate them under a heat lamp. She shivered in the cold. "How can you not be cold?" she asked Seth, who had his gloves off and jacket open.

He laughed. "I'm from Canada. This is mild winter weather for me. If I were working outside, I'd ditch my jacket."

"I'm cold too," Chantal agreed.

"Hang tight, I have an idea." He shoved the last bite of his burger into his mouth and took off. He was back in five minutes and dumped some packets on the table.

"Heat packets. Break them open, like this." He demonstrated. "Slip them in your gloves, pockets, boots. Whatever's cold." He helped Chantal put them in her gloves and down the front of her winter boots.

"Oh." She grinned. "That's so warm. Can we walk around some more?" she begged.

The joy on her daughter's face had Joy agreeing instantly. "Sure, why not? But not much longer," she warned. She didn't have a reason for ending the evening early, she just wanted to reinforce the fact that she was in charge. They took frequent breaks as they toured the vendors. Joy bought herself a lovely hand-knit scarf for almost nothing and let herself be talked into another toque for Chantal. What she would do with it back in California, Joy didn't know, but this was a vacation, and she was doing her best to have fun and stay on budget.

They were passing a small stage when they noticed Jenny climbing the steps. A large group of television cameramen and people with their phones out were gathered in front. The mayor introduced Jenny, who smiled widely at the audience.

Seth leaned close to Joy and whispered, "Do you think she's the benefactor?"

"That would make sense. It seems like she's everywhere. But I've also seen that couple several times since we left the train." She pointed to a middle-aged man and woman wearing matching jackets and hats. "They were in the mall, and at the concert. They're here too. It could be them."

"I hadn't noticed them," Seth said. "You might be right. I wonder why the benefactor wants to remain a secret. You'd think the publicity would be a good thing." He paused. "They had camera crews here, and I saw Jenny on the news last night doing an update on the contestants. I guess Team Bevin made their goal, and I'm assuming we did. I hope." He raised his crossed fingers to reinforce his hopes.

"Seth, Joy, Chantal, can you come up here?"

Joy glanced at Seth, who shrugged. They pushed through the crowd and paused at the base of the stairs. With snowy boots, Joy didn't want to risk Chantal slipping on the stairs.

"Let's have a big hand for team Triple Threat who have successfully met their challenge," Jenny called. The crowd roared and cheered. Cameras focused on them. Joy smiled proudly; they had done this. She'd conquered her fear and gotten through their challenge. After a few other announcements, the mayor stepped on stage.

"Welcome everyone. It's good to see so many locals out tonight. I know that there are several passengers from The Rocky Mountain Christmas Train here. Thank you for coming out." He paused and scanned the crowd. "Usually, I hit the switch and light the tree. But in honor of their success, I'd like to invite Team Triple Threat up on stage to do it for me. Come on up."

"The stairs might be slippery," Joy whispered to Seth.

"Can we go, Mama? Please."

Who was she to deny her daughter this opportunity? "Okay, be careful," she warned.

"I've got this," Seth said. "You ready?" He asked Chantal. When she nodded, he scooped her into his arms and carried her onto the stage. Joy followed behind. He did seem to be one of the good guys.

"Do you have anything to say?" the mayor asked.

Joy swallowed and stepped forward. "We're honored to be here. Thanks to The Rocky Mountain Christmas Train for making this happen for us. Lyons is a lovely town. We're enjoying our visit."

Seth stepped up beside her and slung his arm around her shoulder. "We're thrilled to have passed our challenge and while we wish the other contestants the best, we're hoping we make it through to the end and earn the prize for our charities. I want all of you to know that we wouldn't have gotten this far without the help of Miss Chantal. She's been our cheerleader and has come up with several winning ideas that propelled us along. She also stepped in tonight, by going on stage for the first time in her life, taking the place of an unwell choir member and saving the play. Let's have a big hand for Chantal."

The crowd roared as Joy's heart soared. Her heart blossomed with warmth and caring for Seth. He was an amazing man.

After some quick instructions from the mayor, they counted down, and Chantal hit the switch. The tree quickly lit from bottom to top as the speakers blared *We Wish You a Merry Christmas.*

Chapter Eleven

S eth wasn't entirely certain how it happened, but to his surprise, they were standing just outside the area roped off for the bonfire.

"Can we go warm up?" Chantal asked.

As promised, she'd been the picture of obedience tonight. She'd done well at the lighting and exceptionally on stage. She was adorable and had stolen a piece of his heart. Joy, on the other hand, perplexed him. She was an upbeat woman who obviously cared about her child. She was generous and giving. He'd seen that a few times over the past two days. But she ran hot and cold. One minute she seemed attracted to him, the next she was backing away like he was on fire.

"Please, Mama. I'm getting cold." She didn't whine, she just asked nicely and waited.

Joy looked at her daughter and then at Seth. He shrugged. She was going to decline; it was written all over her face. She leaned close to Seth and raised on her toes. "Will you keep her safe?" she whispered; her breath warm on his cheek. He knew he should answer the question, but for a moment, he was caught up in the warmth of her breath and the desire to kiss her.

"Um. Yes. I'll do my best to keep her out of harm's way." He turned slightly and looked down at Joy. "From my perspective as a firefighter, I'll tell you what I see. firefighterOf course, there's a danger here. There always is when fire is present. But look around, all those people in vests are here to supervise. I've seen at least five local firefighters as well. The crowd is calm. This is about as safe as a bonfire gets. It'll be okay."

She looked at him, her eyes doubtful. He wondered what she saw as she studied his face. After a moment, she nodded. "Thank you." Her voice was filled with gratitude but still held a quiver of nerves. She turned away. "Come on, Chantal. You listen to me, and to Mr. Mathison, okay?"

"Yes." She bounced in place without lifting her crutches from the ground. She had the winter traction spikes firmly dug into the snow.

Chantal's sweet excitement and the trust on Joy's face gave him a funny feeling in his chest. He rubbed at the unfamiliar sensation as they walked to the opening in the ropes surrounding the fire. A uniformed firefighter let them in after consulting a clipboard.

"Limited entry," he explained. "We only allow a set number of people in at once. We ask that you limit your visit to fifteen minutes and to please leave if you see a line forming; that allows us to make room for everyone."

"Thanks," Seth said. "We'll do that."

"Okay, be careful," he warned.

"We will."

Joy led the way. Chantal followed her and Seth brought up the rear. They were able to get right to the chain fence surrounding the fire, and that was at least four feet from the fire to where they were standing. It was a neatly controlled fire and, at this distance, the perfect warmth. He wasn't particularly cold, but the blaze's heat was welcome.

Chantal laughed. "This is ah-may-zing."

Seth had to agree. Joy smiled, but looked unsettled. He could tell every minute they spent here was agony for her. As much as he wanted to fully enjoy the fire, he barely paid attention to it. He kept his eyes open for potential dangers. Running kids, someone slipping, or an over-zealous log throwing could all spell trouble. He wanted to be ready. He had to protect the people he cared for.

Cared for? He blinked several times, but the thought was stuck. He did care for them. How had he come to love the courageous Chantal in only two days? She was a special kid and already dear to him. And Joy? Joy had somehow wormed her way into his heart as well. Love popped into his head. Did he love Joy? Naw, too soon for that, but he knew he was falling.

He'd been in love once before, but she'd left him when he spiraled out of control after his niece's death. Six long months, and a lot of therapy later, he'd regained most of his equilibrium and she'd moved on. Surprisingly, he hadn't missed her too badly. Maybe he'd been in love with the idea of being in love and having a family of his own.

He couldn't help but think that perhaps it was time to start thinking about the future again. Suddenly, he was eager to get home and call his mother and tell her he'd met someone.

Granted, there were a million pitfalls ahead. Not the least of which was the fact that Joy and Chantal lived in California, and he lived in Canada. He pushed the sudden enthusiasm down. He had the rest of the train journey to get to know them better, to figure out if the connection he felt was shared.

He tuned out his thoughts and after a long, slow glance at his companions, focused his attention back on the fire.

Someone to his left threw something at the fire. It hit with an audible thump and burst into an explosion of brightly colored sparks. People screamed and Chantal jerked backward. Seth lunged for her arm to hold her upright. He missed and in what felt like slow motion, she tipped backward and went down. Hard.

Joy screeched and dropped to her knees. "Chantal? Are you okay?" She glared at Seth. "Help me get her up. We're leaving."

"Mama, I'm fine. I was watching the carolers over there. The noise startled me. I'm fine."

"I don't care. Seth, help me," Joy demanded.

He bent and lifted Chantal to her feet, though he was certain she could have done it herself, given the time to do so. "There you go," he said, making sure she had a proper grip on her crutches.

"We're leaving," Joy barked.

Chantal looked crestfallen but didn't argue. Seth was annoyed, but he understood Joy's feelings. "Do you want me to lead or follow?" he asked.

"I'll go first. You make sure she doesn't fall again," Joy growled.

Seth nodded. Chantal gave him a 'my mom is nuts' look but followed her mother out. The silence between them on the way out of the park and in the taxi to the train was arctic cold. Seth's heart shriveled.

"Can we talk?" Seth asked as they crossed the platform to the train.

"No. It's past Chantal's bedtime and I won't leave her alone."

Okay, he could respect that. "What if I found a babysitter?"

"I should just trust some random babysitter?" She gave him a withering stare.

A lesser man would have been defeated. "How about I find someone, and if you approve of them, we spend a few minutes together?" He wasn't above pleading. For all that their relationship ran the gamut from flames to ashes, he wanted to talk to her, see why she was so afraid of giving Chantal an inch, to learn who she was when she wasn't in Mama Bear Mode.

"Maybe," Joy snapped. "If I feel I can trust them."

"Where can I find you when I locate someone?"

She gave him their room number and turned to go.

"Goodnight, Joy. Sleep well, Chantal. Maybe we can see each other tomorrow."

Joy glared at him over her shoulder. One thing was for certain: the woman had spunk. He waved and winked when Chantal looked back at him. She grinned in return.

Joy pushed her hair back and furiously brushed it into a ponytail. She was exhausted. Chantal was in bed reading but showed no signs of going to sleep. Part of her hoped Seth found a suitable sitter.

She couldn't even remember the last time she'd gone out without Chantal. Even if it was with Seth, she could sure use a night out.

How could such a good-looking and helpful man be so infuriating? He made her crazy in more ways than one. She wanted to see more of him, and at the same time hoped never to see his face again. Maybe he'd get off the train now. She snorted at the ridiculous thought. She wasn't about to give up a free train trip and three weeks of free side excursions. Why would he?

"Mama, there's someone at the door."

Really? She hadn't heard a knock. She strode to the door and peered through the peephole. Seth. She might have known. She yanked the door open.

"Hi. You know Maddie, right?" Seth said instead of greeting her. "I ran into her in the lounge car. Chris is sleeping, and she has the night off."

"I'd love to watch Chantal for you," Maddie smiled warmly.

Joy debated with herself. A nurse would be the perfect babysitter. She twisted her lips together and clenched her fists. They were on a train and security guards patrolled the halls at night to make sure there were no uninvited passengers and to watch for potential problems. It would probably be safe.

"I brought my book and some coloring pages for us to do." She pulled a sheaf of papers from her purse. A box of pencil crayons and a few other things clattered to the ground. Joy knelt and picked up a lip balm, a hairbrush, a bottle of spirit gum, and a tin of black shoe polish from the floor and passed them to Maddie, who was picking up other things. Maddie blushed. "Sorry. I carry a lot of stuff. Both mine and Chris's." She shrugged. "I probably should have dumped some of it out, but I wasn't expecting to babysit. Well, what do you think? Can I babysit? I've been missing my sister's kids since I started working for Chris."

"I guess so," Joy decided uncertainly. "Let me grab a sweater." She gave Chantal her cell phone. "Seth's number is in there. Call if you need anything. I won't be long." She kissed her daughter on the cheek and, with a confused heart, followed Seth out of the room.

"Where would you like to go?" he asked.

"The bar," she said emphatically.

"There's a jazz trio in the bar. Is that okay? Or would you prefer the lounge? It's quiet in there tonight, or it was when I left." He'd prefer someplace quiet, but he'd go along with what she chose.

"The lounge, I think. It's closer and after tonight's excitement, I could use some peace and quiet." She ran a mental calculation to see if she dared treat herself to a glass of wine.

"The lounge it is, and drinks are on me." He gestured for her to lead the way.

"I can buy my drink," she said over her shoulder. *What was with macho men?*

"If it's all the same to you, I'd like to buy. As a thank you for a wonderful evening. I've really enjoyed spending time with you and Chantal."

Did he mean that? She enjoyed his company, too. He was kind and solicitous; he didn't bark back when she was upset with him. Chantal adored him. She hadn't drawn a picture for anyone in ages. "Okay. One drink, then I'm back to my room," she warned. She didn't look over her shoulder, but she expected he was grinning.

"Hey, Twyla," Seth greeted the buxom server who was behind the bar tonight. "How's things?"

"Living the dream, Seth. Living the dream."

What did that even mean? Joy wondered.

"How's your husband?" Seth asked.

"He's great. They've moved to a dig in Ethiopia. Some new major discovery." She laughed. "I don't know. He's all about the past. I'm all about the people. Still, I wouldn't trade him for anyone else. What'll you have?"

"Irish coffee for me, please," Seth said. He looked at Joy.

"Can I get that in decaf, please?" she asked. No way could she handle caffeine this late at night. She'd never get any sleep and while they didn't have any set plans tomorrow, she didn't want to be exhausted.

"Sure thing. I'll have to brew a pot. Why don't you find a seat and I'll bring it out to you?" She slid a basket of potato chips and a bowl of dip their way. "Here's a snack. On the house."

"Thanks," Seth said. "Put those drinks on my tab." Outside spending and alcohol were the only items not included in their journey.

Joy looked around the car. It was her first time in this car, though she'd been in several others. Brass trim gleamed in the dim lights. Electric candles glowed on the cloth-covered tables. The seats were a blend of leather chairs and benches. Everything was set up in cozy settings to accommodate groups of two to six. A small tree glowed with red and white lights in the corner. There was a towering display of wrapped gifts in the opposite corner. Some shades were open, and the train's bright Christmas lights shone in the snow. It was probably the most festive place she'd visited in years. Something about it took the edge off her anger and she found herself relaxing. *Were the gifts real? If so, who were they for?*

"You have a tab? I guess you come here a lot," she said, trying to make conversation and snoop without being too rude.

Seth laughed. "Let's see, once the night we boarded, last night, and earlier tonight. I'm a people person. I like watching and talking to them. I've met lifetime friends in the weirdest places."

"Give me an example." She leaned forward and folded her hands on the table.

"I met my neighbor while on vacation in Amsterdam. He's a veterinarian. He came to Canada from Florida to visit the next summer and ended up staying and opening a clinic."

"That's pretty cool. I'm an office manager for a veterinarian. I love it. Animals are easy to talk to." Seth's chuckle warmed her to her toes. "I know you're a firefighter. Is that why you chose the burn unit for your charity?"

His face crinkled up, and he closed his eyes like he was in agony. It was quite apparent that she had hit a nerve. He twisted his napkin between his fingers until it was shredded.

"I don't talk about it much." His voice was deep with emotion. "My niece was killed five years ago in a fire set by an arsonist." He swallowed hard. His Adam's apple bobbed three times.

"Oh, my gosh! I am so sorry." She clasped his hand. "You must have been devastated."

"I was. We all were. We still are. It's tough to keep going. We manage."

He sniffed discreetly, and she thought her heart would break for him. She couldn't imagine how he could continue his job after that sort of trauma. Her admiration of him ratcheted up a notch.

"I hope we can split the money if we win." A thought hit her. "How do we win?" she posed the question. "I mean, we aren't the only ones to complete our task. How are they going to decide? Are there going to be more tasks?"

"I don't know. Those are some things that bother me. The rules are clear, as far as they go, but they don't mention ties or how the final winner is chosen. Or if we can share the prize."

Twyla set their drinks on the table and pulled a sheet from her pocket. "Here's tonight's newsletter." She slid the paper between them.

Joy picked it up. "Oh gosh," she said after she scanned it. "Team Rancy is out. They were caught cheating and were removed from the train. I feel terrible for them."

"Me too. But it's good news for us," his tone was wry.

She jerked her head up to look at him. He shrugged.

"Hey, it's true. I don't really feel bad for them. They knew the rules. I can't imagine why they would cheat. If it were me, I think a failure would be better than the risk of being kicked off the train." He sipped his coffee.

"I agree. If we had failed, we could still stay on the train and enjoy a free trip. I'd much prefer that than to try to win the wrong way."

Seth agreed. They discussed the contest and other passengers for a bit.

She was starting on her second drink when Seth cleared his throat. "I asked you here for a reason."

"I assumed that." She tried not to think back on how many times he'd pushed her limits. She was enjoying the evening and didn't want to ruin it with a fight.

"I wanted to apologize, again, for interfering in how you parent Chantal. I've encouraged her to do things you didn't approve of. I let her take part in the play. She lied. It wasn't her idea, it was mine. I can't let her take the blame. Please don't punish her for my misdeeds. She lied to protect me."

Joy huffed. Another tough parenting call. Did she reprimand her daughter for lying or praise her for standing up for another person? Her shoulders sagged. Probably both, but that was a problem for another day.

"My sister has different rules than you. I don't spend much time with my nieces and nephew. They don't live close." He grimaced. "And I find it hard to be around them. Gwyn's passing stole my confidence and comfort around children. And kids remind me of how much I and my family lost."

"Maybe initially," Joy said. *How could he not know how good he was with kids? He was amazing with Chantal, and he'd done a fabulous job with the kids at the concert.* "You managed perfectly with the choir and got the older kids to take part willingly. I think you have more skills than you know." He was so kind and gentle with the children. He'd be a good father...if he decided to become one. She might be too old to carry another child, but that didn't mean he was too old to start a family, even if he seemed to be her age.

Her mind threw out an image of Seth, Chantal, and herself cuddled around a Christmas tree, opening gifts and laughing like a family. She'd be proud to marry a man like Seth. It was so weird that she was even having such a thought after only knowing him for a few days. Maybe they could spend more time together as the trip progressed. It would be less stressful now that their task was complete.

He really was a great guy, with genuine concern for family and strangers. He had a good job, was community-minded, he was kind and understanding. Okay, she admitted it. He was probably husband material. That he liked Chantal, and she liked him, was a bonus. She was about to suggest spending the day together at their next stop when he spoke.

"Chantal did great today." He sounded proud.

"Yes, she did. She faced a lot of new things, but I wish she hadn't gone on stage. And that fall scared the life out of me." She trembled, thinking of her absolute terror and panic when Chantal slipped by the bonfire.

"She wasn't hurt, and she wasn't close enough to be in danger," Seth placated.

"That's not the point," she snapped, slamming her mug down on the table. Coffee and whipped topping splashed over the rim and ran down her hand. *Didn't he care about the risks she'd taken?*

"Okay. What is the point? Help me understand." His calm tone sent her anger skyrocketing.

"The point is that she's my daughter, not yours. You don't get to put her in danger." She clenched her teeth until her jaw ached. It was a wonder she didn't crack her teeth.

"First, she was in no danger on stage. She walked and talked. Things she does every day. Second, we did what you wanted at the mall. I kept her safe by carrying her down the escalator. You agreed to the winter fair and the bonfire. Those are on you, not me. I was there, yes. But you agreed. I helped her when she needed help and, aside from slipping, she wasn't in any danger at any point. Maybe you're being over-protective."

"Over-protective?" she screeched. She ignored the curious stares her elevated voice brought their way. "She's my child. The only one I'll ever have. I can't afford insurance. Do you know what it would cost me if she were seriously hurt?" She didn't wait for a reply. "She's fragile and needs protection from a harsh world." *How could he not understand this? He'd lost someone dear to him, so he, of all people, should get where she was coming from.*

"She's not fragile," Seth disagreed calmly. "She's fully capable of doing almost anything. Don't you think she's ready to try new things? Sure, she'll need to be extra cautious under certain circumstances, but she's a normal child except for her crutches."

"You know nothing about it." She trembled in anger. "Mind your own business." She jerked up from the table and glared down at him. Her height over him gave her the strength for one last shot. "I was going to ask you on a date tomorrow to get to know you better, but that train's left the track. I know all I need to know. Don't talk to me or my daughter again." Head held high; she strode from the car.

Out of sight of Seth and the curious bystanders, she stumbled down the hall and locked herself in a public bathroom. How could she have been so wrong about him?

"Damn you, Seth Mathison."

She sobbed until she had no tears, rinsed her face, and stared into the mirror.

If he was so awful, why did she feel like she'd just lost half her heart?

Rocky Mountain
Christmas Train

Chapter Twelve

S eth couldn't sleep. Tired of tossing and turning, he headed for the forward observation car, the place where he'd been teamed up with Joy and Chantal. At two a.m. he expected the car to be empty. The small counter where they prepped drinks was closed up tight, the lights were off, but a few electric candles glowed in the near dark. It wasn't fully dark because the train's Christmas lights reflected off the snow outside.

A lone figure sat in the corner. He turned to go, not wanting to disturb their solitude.

"You can stay," a voice called out. "Join me. I'm just having tea before I go to bed."

He walked closer. Bruce, the bartender, sat with his feet on the bench across from him. His normally neat blond hair was mussed, and his work tie undone. "Little late to be up," Bruce said.

"I could say the same to you," Seth chuckled, though he didn't feel particularly jolly.

"Late shift today. Closed up at one-thirty. I just finished tidying up and needed a moment to unwind." He shifted his feet and nodded for Seth to sit. "Congrats on the win, mate." His Australian accent was heavier than usual.

"Thanks."

"Want a drink? I could open the bar for you."

"I'd take another," a thirty-something bearded man sitting alone at an adjacent table called. Seth looked at him. Davyn Kayne, the poet, frowned back.

"Mr. Kayne. Why don't you join us?" he offered. His sister was a huge fan of the somewhat reclusive poet's work. Maybe he could get her an autograph.

The slightly rumpled gentleman joined them. They chatted about the weather while Bruce fixed the man a drink.

"Last one, Mr. Kayne," Bruce said in his heavy Aussie accent. "You sure you don't want one, Mr. Mathison?"

"Naw. I'm good." The last thing Seth needed was to start drinking when he was stressed. Too many firefighters used alcohol as a coping mechanism. He did have an occasional drink, but never when he was stressed. He sat across from Bruce.

"Excitement over possibly winning the big prize keeping you awake?"

Seth snorted. "I wish."

"Woman troubles?"

"Those are my options?" Seth said somewhat sarcastically. "Excitement and women?"

"Well, could be work, but you're on vacation."

Seth leaned his head back and closed his eyes. After a long silence, he said. "Why are women so confusing?"

"Don't ask me, mate. I've been aboard for five days, including training. I've got three chicks chasing me, and the one I like won't even look at me. Dunno, mate, chicks are weird."

"Not weird," Seth countered, trying to assemble his thoughts. "Complicated." He nodded at the mental discovery. "We just need to unlock the puzzle."

Bruce laughed. "Right." So much sarcasm in one word. "You and Joy then? What's up? That kid getting in your way?"

"Not even close. I adore Chantal."

"And you've got the hots for the mom?" Bruce took a swig from his large mug.

"I like Joy. We've clashed a few times, but she's easy to be with. She..." He struggled to find an explanation for how he felt. He'd never felt anything even close. And the one experience that had felt similar sure hadn't been an overnight thing.

It was like love at first sight.

Whoa! No!

Maybe?

Something had sparked in his chest when he saw Joy on the platform. It had grown over the hours they spent together. He wanted to explore that and see where it went.

"I messed up."

Bruce nodded, but didn't offer any words of wisdom. Seth appreciated the silence. It was comfortable, like Bruce understood what he was going through. He needed to talk about this, and it was a ridiculous time to call anyone he knew.

"What do you do when you say something incredibly unfeeling and stupid?"

"Apologize?"

Seth groaned and scraped his hand across his midnight whiskers. They were well beyond a five o'clock shadow. He'd already known he needed to apologize, but hearing it from another man's lips was annoying. "I guess I better."

A weight lifted off his soul. Having a plan was freeing. Okay, not a plan exactly, but an idea of what came next. He just had to figure out how to grovel meaningfully.

"What are you going to do about the ladies?" he asked Bruce.

"Keep on saying no and keep on asking for dates. I guess."

Mr. Kayne finished his drink and left. Bruce and Seth talked for another twenty minutes until Bruce got up. "I'm out. I need some sleep. Cocoa duty in the caboose tomorrow. We're open for cocoa and Santa visits from noon to four. It's gonna be a rough go."

"Have a good night," he said as Bruce walked away.

Seth sat in the near dark, regretting his big mouth. He felt terrible for confronting Joy about her parenting. She was right; it wasn't any of his business, but at the same time, she was smothering her daughter. Chantal had mentioned not having any aunts or uncles. He knew her father ditched at her diagnosis. That left Joy alone. Sometimes you needed family or friends to tell you when you were messing things up. He didn't regret telling Joy, but he regretted the way he'd done it.

He fisted his hands in self-censure.

Mostly, he regretted losing her friendship and what he had been hoping might turn into a deeper, longer-lasting relationship. He was falling for her. He had been since her first staunch defense of her daughter on the platform.

Despite knowing he wouldn't sleep, he returned to his cabin and tried to rest.

Bleary-eyed and exhausted, Seth was surprised to see Chantal sitting alone in the dining car the next morning. Ignoring Joy's orders, he greeted her. "Good morning, Chantal. Any plans for today?"

"No. Mama has a headache. She's sleeping in."

"And you left without permission?" He raised one eyebrow in question. There would be trouble if she had defied her mother's orders. He couldn't believe Joy would let her daughter come here alone.

"No. She said I could. Miss Jenny is watching me." She pointed toward the far corner where Jenny, still wearing her Mrs. Claus outfit, was talking to a small group of staff members in low secretive tones. She kept glancing around as if to ensure nobody was listening.

"They're telling secrets," Chantal said. "Mama says secrets are rude."

"Sometimes they are. Usually they are," he corrected himself. "But it is Christmas, and that's a time for special secrets. Like what gift you bought someone or a wonderful surprise you have planned. I'll bet Miss Jenny is planning a surprise."

"Do you think she's the benef..." she stumbled on the word benefactor. "Did she plan this trip?"

"Maybe. But it's hard to tell. There are hundreds of people on this train and we don't know if the benefactor is even here. They could be somewhere else entirely. Remember yesterday? Think about how many people we saw at the play. Jenny, the people in the matching coats, Nurse Maddie, and Chris, the bald guy with the fake fur coat. The lady who wears the big sweater with the dog team on the back. It could be any of them, or somebody else."

"I suppose." She sounded totally defeated.

"Maybe we'll find out at the end of the trip. Plus, we can watch for clues all month. There are almost three weeks left on this trip. I'll bet we can figure it out by the end." He grinned, though it hurt to see Chantal so despondent about not knowing. "Cheer up and enjoy your day."

"Can you sit with me? I don't like sitting alone. It feels weird." Her cheeks pinkened adorably and something in her eyes reminded him of Joy's fear for her daughter. Mother and daughter were so much alike that it made his chest hurt.

He hesitated. He didn't want to go against Joy's wishes, even if they felt unreasonable.

"Please." She blinked up at him, tears in her eyes.

"Okay." He slid in opposite her.

"I hear Santa is taking visits today. He'll be in the rear observation car. Maybe Jenny can take you to see him." He pulled out his phone. "He'll be doing it after we stop for the day."

"Maybe Mama will get up soon. I'm supposed to eat and get Miss Jenny to take me back to my room." She toyed with her fork, stirring the scrambled egg on her plate. "I don't want to sit all day. I want to do stuff."

Her plea was hard to resist. "Let's just eat and see what happens. We can take our time. I've got all day."

He ordered black coffee and the Mountain Man breakfast special. Three eggs, three sausages, and three slices of bacon on a waffle, with a side order of fruit and rye toast. He'd been so nervous about the contest that he'd eaten very little all day yesterday, though he had tried. He worked hard physically and normally had an enormous appetite. The delicious treats from the food truck were not enough to sustain a man his size.

He thought about his nieces and nephew and wondered if she liked dogs. "Want to see a picture of my puppy?"

"Yes, please!"

He pulled out his phone and scrolled to one of his rescue mutt. Pugster had shaggy black and white hair with weird brown paws. He was patchy and looked rather like he'd been through a blender. Despite his unfortunate appearance, he was the best dog he'd ever had.

"This is Pugster. I call him Pugs. He's kind of the fire station dog. He's mine, but he goes with me to work and hangs out in the hall when I'm on calls."

"Where is he? Isn't he lonely? I'd be lonely if Mama wasn't around. 'Cause I don't have a dad."

"Sorry about your dad." Her sadness broke his heart. "Pugs is staying with my neighbor. They're great friends." He scrolled again. "Here he is with my nieces and nephew. That's Jada, Marnie, and Ryan. If you swipe, you can see more pictures of them."

She scrolled through pictures for a few minutes, commenting on them. He wasn't worried about her seeing anything she shouldn't. "Who is this?" She turned the phone so he could see.

He swallowed hard. "That's Gwyn. She was my niece. She's gone to heaven."

"How did she die?"

God, he'd never get used to that question. His eyes burned and his throat tightened. "She died in a fire."

Chantal's eyes lit with understanding. "That's why you picked the burn place." She patted his hand, exactly as her mother had. His heart swelled. "I think she's in heaven with my gramma and grampa and they're watching us and keeping us safe," she declared matter-of-factly.

"I sure hope you're right."

Something jittery inside Seth settled down and an unfamiliar calm washed over him. There was an absolute rightness to being with Chantal. With sudden clarity, he realized it was exactly what he felt around Joy.

Peace, contentment, and absolute love. Granted, it was early for that, but he vowed to win Joy's forgiveness, and from there...well he had the rest of the trip to convince her he was worth the risk. All he had to do was get her talking to him.

They ate and chatted while Jenny dealt with her staff. He was lingering over his coffee, and Chantal over her juice, when Jenny bustled up to the table, her Mrs. Claus glasses crooked and her wig askew.

"I have to go see Santa. Did you want to come?" she asked Chantal.

"I know he's not real Santa," Chantal said. "But Mama says he knows real Santa. So yes!" She fist-pumped the air and scooted out of the bench with amazing speed.

"Mind if I tag along?" Seth asked. "Maybe I'll get a chance to tell Santa what I want for Christmas." He grinned at Jenny and winked, after being certain Chantal wouldn't notice.

"Sure, tag along. Since it's in the caboose, why don't I run ahead, and you follow with Chantal?" There was an underlying subtext in her voice. She was a busy woman and having to wait for a girl on crutches would slow her down.

"Is that okay with you, Chantal?" Seth asked.

She grinned and nodded. "Yup."

Jenny bolted, and the duo set off toward the caboose. The slight swaying motion of the train didn't seem to bother Chantal much. He was extra vigilant as they passed between cars. When they reached a public area near the center of the train, he said. "I could use a rest."

Chantal turned and gave him a pinched look. "I'm not tired." Implying that there was something wrong with him if he was. "I want to see Santa."

She didn': say it, but her exasperation at his suggestion was clear. "Carry on then. I'll manage." Truthfully, his body wasn't tired, but his nerves were stressed beyond anything he'd ever experienced. How did Joy handle her nerves, living like this day in and day out? His respect for her grew. He also admired Chantal's stamina. It couldn't be easy to walk with her crutches. Pride for her abilities filled his heart.

Rocky Mountain Christmas Train

Chapter Thirteen

J oy wasn't sleeping. She wished she could doze off, but her heart
   ached too badly. She fluffed her pillow and rolled onto her left
side. Closing her eyes against the morning sun peeking around the
roll blinds, she found herself wondering how it was possible that she
felt worse after a fight with Seth than she did when her ex abandoned
them. She still wasn't over her betrayal at being ditched by her ex.

Maybe she never would be. But this pain from her fight with Seth felt like losing a loved one.

She studied their relationship and what she'd learned about him from all sides. He'd never been less than kind. Though they didn't need help, he'd stuck up for them on the platform. He'd encouraged Chantal to try new things. Not that she needed the push.

She winced at the realization that he'd been right and that she was more capable than Joy believed. "Am I holding on too tight?" she muttered aloud as she tried to get comfortable again.

"Oh, dang it." She threw the covers back and got up. She popped a couple of pain tablets for her headache and climbed into the shower. One of today's stops was a petting zoo and pony rides. Chantal was dying to ride a pony. Initially, she had said no. Now she wondered if there was a way to make it happen.

She slipped into a thick pair of black leggings and a red sweater with a snowman on the front. Completing the outfit, she added her light jacket and tall leather boots. She stared at herself in the full-length mirror on the back of the door. Her face was pinched and nervous.

"What are you going to do, Joy?" She wrinkled her nose. "He's right. You are a helicopter parent. You'd wrap Chantal in bubble wrap if you could." Her exhaustion amplified her wrinkles, and she had bags under her eyes. She looked fifty-four, not forty-four. She used the tips of her fingers to pull the sides of her eyes back, removing the wrinkles. "If only they'd stay like this."

She should find her daughter and make plans for the day.

"You should go find Seth and apologize for losing it on him." She frowned at her reflection. "Why does it matter? We're incompatible, no matter how many admirable traits he has." But she'd been rude, and she would apologize.

Her phone binged. Jenny and her daughter were headed to the rear observation car. She'd meet them there. Whistling *I'll be Home for Christmas*, she locked her cabin and headed for the rear of the train.

When she arrived, the car was chaos. Deep snow covered everything. Jenny scurried around, helping scoop up snow and toss it outside. "We have to get this fixed," she declared loudly. "We've only got half an hour until we stop and we have hundreds of kids booked to see Santa."

Joy peered around looking for Chantal. Where was her daughter? Panic rose in her chest, choking off her ability to breathe. Had Jenny left Chantal alone?

"Breathe," she whispered to herself. "We're on a moving train. She can't go anywhere." She tried to catch Jenny's eye, but she was too busy.

Stunned and immobile, she clenched and unclenched her fists. Breaking free of the terror that gripped her she strode into the disaster.

"Mama!"

She whirled toward the voice. Her heart thundered. Chantal stood in the doorway with Seth right behind her. *Thank heavens Chantal hadn't been alone.*

"Mama, you're awake!" She hurried to Joy's side. Seth followed hesitantly behind her.

"Hey, kiddo." They shared a warm hug.

"As you can see, Jenny had an emergency. I was in the dining car, and she asked me to accompany Chantal here. I hope you don't mind."

She glanced at the chaos behind her. She had no idea what happened, but it looked like someone had left the car doors open during last night's blowing snow. Jenny had left Chantal behind, but it was with a responsible adult.

"Thank you, Seth." She smiled warmly. "I appreciate it." He'd gone out of his way for them. Something lifted inside her.

"Oh, Joy. You're here. I am so sorry I had to leave Chantal. I hope it's okay." Jenny rushed to their side. "I have a mess here." She waved around the car. "Nothing that a good cleaning won't fix, but it's a lot to do in a short time. I'll see you later?" It was a clear suggestion that they should leave.

"You bet."

"Can I make a suggestion?" Seth asked.

Jenny blinked like she'd just realized he was there. "Um? Sure?"

"You could set Santa up in the middle observation car. It's beautifully decorated. It's got two doors. You could funnel families in one door and out the other." He paused. "There's room for the camera, an elf, and the supplies. Move the coffee table and put Santa on the high-backed sofa. Close the blinds, and you've got Christmas heaven."

"That's brilliant." She gave a sharp whistle. "Okay everyone, new plan." Her elfish staff scurried into action, toting boxes and supplies out of the room.

"Step out of the doorway, honey," Joy said, as they moved out of the way. In moments, nobody was left except three people with small shovels and cleaning rags.

"Can I buy you a coffee?" Seth asked.

She had to apologize, so why not? "Sure. I'd like that. I think I'm ready for breakfast."

"Mama, it's almost lunch," Chantal declared.

"Fine, I need lunch." She poked her daughter's shoulder. The kid was smart, and sometimes, just a hint of a smart Alec.

"Excellent. Should we eat on the train, or wait until we stop? I don't think we're far out of town."

"I'd rather eat now. There are some things I'd like to do in town." Ugh. She sounded so stiff and formal. "If it's okay, can we just go to the dining car?"

Seth followed behind Joy, who followed Chantal down the hall. Joy imagined they looked a bit like a train, or maybe a parade. Finally, they entered the dining car. She'd passed through it earlier but hadn't looked. She'd been too intent on finding Chantal. The seats were cushiony, and the tables were covered with cloths. Hm. She'd expect that at night, but not around noon. There was an elegant Christmas vibe. Lights and pine garland swags decorated the walls and hung over the windows.

There was a serious looking man with a short beard sitting alone in the far corner scribbling in a notebook. She wracked her brain, trying to figure out where she knew him from. "Isn't that Davyn Kayne the poet?" she whispered at last.

"It sure is. We talked briefly the other night. I believe he was wrapped up in some big lawsuit, though I can't remember for sure. I wonder if he's a passenger or a contestant."

Joy chuckled. "Time will tell."

She looked around, trying to find the best place to sit. Many of the tables were full, but there was an empty one in the far corner. "Let's sit there." She pointed discreetly. "Beside that woman with the cell phone." The woman she pointed to seemed to be playing a matching game and studiously avoiding being caught looking at Davyn. *Interesting. Did they know each other? Or was she attracted to the man? He was attractive in a rumpled sort of way.*

Outside, the winter landscape flowed past. The train was making a leisurely run to allow time for all the contestants to compete. Farms with inflatable ornaments on their snowy lawns. Enormous trees with lights and oversized holiday ornaments. A life-size nativity scene complete with live cows. The whole thing reminded her of the goodness, kindness, and generosity of the spirit. It was a time for love and forgiveness.

Suddenly, her spirits lifted. If he accepted her apology, they could see where their relationship went.

She ordered lunch, while Seth and Chantal ordered drinks and cookies. The trio sat staring at each other. Chantal looked from one to the other and back again. "Did you guys get in a fight?" she asked. She squinted at them, worry in her eyes.

"Yes," Seth said before Joy could answer. "I was rude to your mom, and stuck my nose into her business when I shouldn't have." He turned to look Joy right in the eye.

It was all she could do not to look away. He wasn't the only one who had messed up.

"Joy, I am sorry that I stuck my nose into your business. You know what's right for your family. I apologize. I'll try to do better in the future."

Apologize too. Get to know him. There are almost three full weeks left on the train. They could get to know each other better. Date a little. Who knows what will happen?

Her heart warmed. If he accepted her apology, they could see where their relationship went. Explore the weird, light sensation in her chest.

"Thanks. I accept your apology." She swallowed the lump of emotion in her throat. "I'm sorry I lost my temper. You were right. Maybe I'm over-protective. Chantal is capable of more than I care to admit."

Chantal gasped. "Does this mean I can ride the ponies?"

A small laugh burst out. "It means we'll go see if there is a safe way for you to ride. I'm worried you don't have the strength in your legs to stay upright. But we'll go and check. Okay?"

"Yay!"

Seth said. "Now that we're back with a clean slate between us..." he paused like he was nervous. "If you don't mind, I would love to accompany you ladies to the petting zoo. I've heard there are reindeer. I wonder if we could ride them. I've always wanted a reindeer ride."

"I don't know about that," Joy said. "Let's start with the zoo and see how it goes."

"One other thing," Seth smiled a nervous smile.

They had just made up. What in the world could he be nervous about? "What's that?" Joy asked, her curiosity rising.

"I've made a decision."

She raised her eyebrows in question.

"If we win this thing, though I don't know how they make the final decision.... If we win and we don't get to split the prize and only one of us gets it, I want you to have it for your charity. Cerebral palsy doesn't get as much attention as a children's hospital. Take the prize. Assuming we win, it's yours."

"I can't do that," she said. Shame filled her heart. He didn't know the truth.

"Yes, you can. I insist."

"Seth, I can't." She didn't want to start arguing again when they'd just made up. "It's too generous."

"Why not? If only one can win, I want it to be you."

She blinked back tears. "Because," she whispered, "I'm the charity. Okay?"

He looked stunned. "What does that mean?" he asked after a long, painful pause.

"It means that I'm up to my forehead in debt from Chantal's care. Medical care in the U.S. is insane. I submitted myself as the charity with the Cerebral Palsy Association getting what's left after I pay off my medical bills." Her face heated, and she stared at the table, blinking rapidly to clear tears of mortification.

His hand slid across the table, and he cupped her chin. It was warm from holding his coffee. Gently, he raised her chin until she saw the concerned expression on his face.

"Joy, there is no shame in owing money for medical care. I'm blessed with free health care. I want you to take the money. If the benefactor thinks supporting you is a worthy cause, who am I to argue? If we win and aren't allowed to share the prize between our charities, I'm changing my charity to yours. End of discussion."

"Why?" she demanded, torn between hating his pity and adoring his generosity.

"Why?" He chuckled. "That's the simple part. Because I like you, Joy Spencer. A lot. And I adore Chantal. You're both teaching me that having an iced-over heart isn't a good thing. I'm learning to care again, all because of you. You are a very special woman, and I want to get to know you better."

To Joy, it felt like he was leaving things unsaid. But why wouldn't he? They barely knew each other at all. But she did know that he was a great guy, and she was falling for him. He was a wonderful man. Kind and generous. Good to her and caring of Chantal. He wanted the best for her daughter. He was the kind of man she should have married. She'd take the next three weeks to get to know him and see if her heart was right, that she was falling in love with him.

"Thank you, Seth. It would mean the world to me to be debt-free. Well, I'd still have the mortgage on my condo, and my car payment." She laughed. "But no medical bills would make our lives so much easier. "Thank you."

"Can we go ride the reindeer now?" Chantal asked.

Joy and Seth shared a long laugh. "Sure thing, kiddo," Joy said. Love and hope for the future blossomed in her heart.

Preview

Are you curious who the mysterious benefactor of this incredible train trip is? Who could possibly have enough money to fund a month-long trip for one hundred contestants and provide a twenty-five-thousand-dollar prize? Wonder why they'd be inspired to run such a contest.

Are you wondering why Davyn Kayne is aboard? Wonder what his story is? Check out the next wonderful story, *A Verse to Christ-*

mas, written by Roxy Boroughs, as she follows The Rocky Mountain Christmas Train on its exciting journey toward Canada.

The Rocky Mountain Christmas Train Series

Author's Note:

Except for one quick trip between London and Paris, I've never ridden on a train. An overnight trip through the mountains is on my bucket list. But I fear I'll need a winning lottery ticket to make that dream a reality.

A couple of instances in this story come out of my personal life. When I was in grade eleven, I competed for and won the title of Snow Queen in the small town where I lived. My performance piece was playing the piano. I did, indeed, set the piano stool on my floor-length dress. I tore a tiny hole in the seam. Luckily, it held up for the entire night.

The second instance comes from my dear brother, who, during a church concert chose to exercise his irreverent nature and fall on his knees during a choir event. Unlike Seth and Joy, my mother was not amused.

About Katie O'Connor

Best-selling author Katie O'Connor lives in Calgary, Alberta, Canada. She married her high school sweetheart and is living her happily ever after. She is the mother of two grown daughters and is extremely proud of her five grandchildren.

She is the founder of The Write Chicks, a private romance writers' group set up with the sole purpose of supporting each other's writing career. Currently, she is past president of the Calgary Association of the Romance Writers of America. In the past, she's been their secretary and has also served on the organizing committee for When Words Collide, a reader and writer conference in Calgary, Alberta. In 2025 she will be a Story Coach for the Alexandra Writer's Center Society in Calgary.

Katie's career path has been long and twisted, with most of her life devoted to her family. She's been a waitress, chambermaid, cashier, store manager, as well as a lab and X-ray technician. She's been a small business owner and is an avid quilter and crafter.

She's dabbled in writing since high school because something drives her to create stories. She swears it's impossible for her NOT to write. Unsatisfied with one genre, Katie writes contemporary romance, erotic romance, fantasy/paranormal romance, romantic suspense, and erotica.

She believes in all things magical, including dragons, fairies, UFOs, ghosts, and house pixies. But most of all she believes in love, romance, and hope.

Where to Find Katie

Website: https://katieohwrites.com
Email: http://katie@katieohwrites.com
Newsletter Sign-up: http://eepurl.com/Q2nRr
Facebook: http://www.facebook.com/katieohwrites
BookBub: https://www.bookbub.com/profile/katie-o-connor
Instagram: https://www.instagram.com/katieohwrites/
Goodreads: https://www.goodreads.com/author/show/5362469.
Katie_O_Connor

Books by Katie O'Connor

A Silver Fox Christmas Box Set
Heart's Haven:
Running Home
Building Trust
Saving Grace
Heart's Haven Box Set
Three Moon Falls:
Fire Magic
Water Magic
Earth Magic
Stand Alone Books:
Carly's Heart
Matchmaker Christmas
Cupid's Charm
Gingerbread Dreams
Christmas in Silver Creek
Fake Dating at Half Moon Bay
Sleigh Bells Inn
Hearts in the Spotlight
To a Tea
Bulletproof Heat
Protecting Josie
Rekindled Fire
Coming Soon:
Ticket to Her Heart
Air Magic

www.ingramcontent.com/pod-product-compliance
Lightning Source LLC
Chambersburg PA
CBHW022029170626
46808CB00003B/1113